The boy crawled into the hole. He was different from the people who'd been here before. He didn't shout and grab. He didn't bring blazing lights.

Still, I was wary. This boy could be dangerous. But even though I was frightened of him, I also felt an urge to get up and trot over to him. It was strange, but part of me wanted to be close to a human.

This human.

Also by
W. Bruce Cameron

Bailey's Story

Cooper's Story

Ellie's Story

Lacey's Story

Lily's Story

Max's Story

Molly's Story

Shelby's Story

Toby's Story

Lily to the Rescue

Lily to the Rescue: Two Little Piggies

Lily to the Rescue: The Not-So-Stinky Skunk

Lily to the Rescue: Dog Dog Goose

Lily to the Rescue: Lost Little Leopard

Lily to the Rescue: The Misfit Donkey

Lily to the Rescue: Foxes in a Fix

Lily to the Rescue: The Three Bears

Zeus: Water Rescue

A PUPPY TALE

Bella's Story

W. Bruce Cameron

Illustrations by
Richard Cowdrey

STARSCAPE

Tor Publishing Group
New York

BELLA'S STORY

Copyright © 2020 by W. Bruce Cameron
Illustrations © 2020 by Richard Cowdrey
Reading and Activity Guide copyright © 2020 by Tor Books

A Starscape Book
Published by Tom Doherty Associates / Tor Publishing Group
120 Broadway
New York, NY 10271

www.tor-forge.com

The Library of Congress has cataloged the hardcover edition as follows:

Names: Cameron, W. Bruce, author.
Title: Bella's story : a puppy tale / W. Bruce Cameron ; illustrations by Richard Cowdrey.
Description: First edition. | New York : Starscape, a Tom Doherty Associates Book, 2020. | Series: A puppy tale
Identifiers: LCCN 2022277753 (print) | ISBN 9781250212764 (hardcover) | ISBN 9781250212740 (ebook)
Subjects: LCSH: Human–animal relationships—Juvenile fiction. | Dogs—Juvenile fiction. | Voyages and travels—Juvenile fiction. | Survival—Juvenile fiction. | LCSHAC: Dogs— Fiction. | Human–animal relationships—Fiction. | Other subjects: JUVENILE FICTION— Animals—Dogs. | Dogs. | Human–animal relationships. | Survival. | Voyages and travels. | LCGFT: Junior fiction. | Animal fiction. | Fiction. | Juvenile works.
Classification: LCC PZ7.C1442 Bel 2020 (print) | DDC 813/.6—dc23
LC record available at https://lccn.loc.gov/2022277753

ISBN 978-1-250-21277-1 (trade paperback)

Our books may be purchased in bulk for promotional, educational, or business use. Please contact your local bookseller or the Macmillan Corporate and Premium Sales Department at 1-800-221-7945, extension 5442, or by email at MacmillanSpecialMarkets@macmillan.com.

First Starscape Paperback Edition: 2023

Printed in the United States of America

10 9 8 7 6 5 4 3 2 1

For Shelby, Rhedyn, and Ellery Owen

Bella's Story

A Puppy Tale

1

From the beginning, there were cats.

Cats everywhere.

I couldn't really see them, even though my eyes were open. When they were nearby, all I was aware of was shifting shapes in the darkness.

But I could smell them, just as I smelled my mother and her milk. Just as I smelled my brothers and sisters, close to me in a squirming, wiggling pile.

I didn't know they were cats at first, of course. I only knew that they were close to me, and that for some reason they didn't try to nurse alongside me. I was grateful for that—it was difficult enough to find a place to feed at my mother's side with my littermates always shoving me around.

Later on, I discovered that cats were their own kind of animals, small and fast and graceful. Many of them

were tiny and young and had their own mothers, which explained why they didn't try to nurse from mine.

We all lived together in a cool, dark home. There was dirt under my paws, and the dirt was full of old, dry smells. Above, there was a ceiling of wood. Whenever my mother got to her feet, her tail made a perfect upright curve that reached halfway to that ceiling.

The only light that entered our home came from a small square hole at the far end, too far away for me to crawl and investigate. Through that hole came astounding smells of things that were cold and alive and wet, things that were even more delightful than the smells of dirt and cats and dogs in the home that I knew.

Sometimes a shadow would flit across the hole and then an exciting, delicious odor would fill the air. The cats would scamper toward this smell. My mother always stood up, shook off a puppy or two, and went with them.

My brothers and sisters and I would huddle together and squeak until she returned. Her mouth and muzzle smelled fascinating—not like milk, and yet like food. We'd lick her frantically. She'd lick us back, and I could feel that she was content.

I was very curious about what might lie on the other side of the hole. But whenever I tried to crawl toward it, my mother would push me back with her nose.

So I mostly kept to the small hollow in the dirt where I had been born. As my legs grew stronger and I could keep my eyes open for longer and longer stretches of time, I played with my brothers and sisters—wonderful

games like Chase-Me and Is-This-Your-Tail-Or-Mine? And sometimes I played with the cats.

There was one cat family who lived nearby with two kittens—one dark, one light. Kittens played different games than my littermates, like Stalk-Me or Pounce-and-Run or Curl-Up-and-Purr. Sometimes I was irritated by the way they played. I wanted to climb on their backs and chew on their necks, but they couldn't seem to get the hang of this. They would just go limp whenever I tried it, and then leap away as soon as I let go. Or they'd wrap their entire bodies around my snout and bat at my face with tiny, sharp claws.

But mostly the kittens were fun, and very good at Chase-Me. Their mother was a big, friendly creature who sometimes licked my ears or cheeks. I thought of her as Mother Cat.

After a game with my kitten friends, my own mother would come to find me. She'd pick me up by the loose skin on the back of my neck and carry me back to where I belonged. She'd drop me in a pile of brothers and sisters, who would sniff me all over. They didn't seem to care for the smell of cat. I couldn't understand why.

That was my life—my mother, my littermates, my cat friends, my wonderful home, and the mystery of the hole that someday, I was sure, I would explore.

One day I was nursing drowsily, my brothers and sisters next to me, when all of a sudden my mother

lunged to her feet. She moved so quickly that my legs were lifted off the ground before I dropped off and fell into a heap.

I knew instantly that something very bad was happening.

A panic spread through our home. Cats scampered toward the back of the den, away from the square hole, some carrying kittens in their mouths. My littermates and I scrambled toward our mother, crying for her, frightened because she was frightened.

Beams of powerful light burst in through the hole. They dazzled my eyes. I had never known anything so bright. Strange sounds came from the other side of those lights.

"There's, like, a hundred cats under this porch!"

"Look, see those bowls? Somebody's been feeding them!"

My mother panted, backing away. We all did our best to stay with her, begging her with our tiny voices not to leave us. Her ears lay flat against her head. All of her attention focused on whatever was making these sounds and flashing these lights.

"Well, we can't knock down a house with a whole cat colony in the crawl space."

"Not just cats. See?" The light swung over my mother. "A dog, too. Looks like a pit bull."

"But we have to stay on schedule. We're supposed to start building in a month."

"I know. I'll have to call somebody."

The beams of light flickered around our home once more, and then went out. The sense of danger faded. My mother came back to us, and my brothers and sisters and I huddled around her and nursed. Milk was warmth and safety and life, so I knew everything was all right.

Around us, cats came out of the shadows. Kittens darted and pounced. When I was done nursing, I'd find my kitten friends and Mother Cat.

Whatever had happened to cause the panic was over.

A few days later, I was playing with Mother Cat's kittens when everything went wrong.

There was light again, but this time not just a few beams. It was a blazing explosion that turned everything bright. I froze, not sure what I should do.

Sounds came from outside the square hole. "Get the nets ready. When they run, they're going to do it all at once!"

"We're set!"

Three large beings wiggled in behind the light. These were the first humans I had ever seen. Even though the light and the noises were alarming, something deep inside me was interested, too. I almost wanted to run toward the people as they crawled into the den.

But I didn't. I stayed still.

"Got one!"

A male cat screeched and hissed. I stared in sur-

prise as Mother Cat seized one of my kitten friends by the scruff of the neck, carrying him away. Cats were fleeing and wailing.

Where was my mother? I couldn't see her; I couldn't even smell her over the scent of frightened cats and invading humans. Then I felt sharp teeth at the back of my neck, and my body went limp. It happened automatically; I didn't even have to think about it.

Mother Cat had me, her teeth gentle but firm on the loose skin at the back of my neck. She dragged me deep into the shadows. There was a stone wall in the back of our den, split by a large crack. She squeezed me through the crack into a small, tight space and set me down with her kittens, curling up around us all.

The two young cats were completely silent. Mother Cat was as well. I did what they did, lying still, not moving, not making a sound.

More noise came from outside.

"There's a litter of puppies here, too!"

"Hey, get that one!"

"Come on, kitty. We're not going to hurt you. We're here to help."

"There's the mother dog."

"She's terrified. Careful she doesn't bite you."

"Here, puppy. Here, puppy. They're so little!"

I heard my mother barking urgently. I knew what that meant—I should go to her! But Mother Cat pressed against me, keeping me still.

The barking and yowling and hissing, and the

strange noises made by the humans, went on for a long time. But eventually they faded away.

The smells of angry, frightened cat faded away, too. After a while I slept.

And when I woke up, my mother was gone.

2

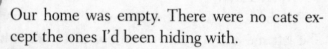Our home was empty. There were no cats except the ones I'd been hiding with.

And no dogs, either.

I went over to the hollow in the dirt where I had snuggled with my brothers and sisters and had sucked milk from my mother. It still smelled like my family, but they were gone. A miserable, lonely feeling rose up inside me as I sniffed the dirt. I could not hold back a whimper.

Mother Cat and the kittens made their way to the small, crumpled piece of cloth that I thought of as their home. Frantic, I hurried over to Mother Cat and nudged her with my nose. Where was my dog mother? Where was my family? What had happened?

Mother Cat sniffed me all over. She licked at my face. Then she lay down. The kittens burrowed into her side.

Mother Cat gazed at me, and I felt her concern. She wanted to take care of me, and I needed to be taken care of. I needed a mother, and now, it seemed, that mother was Mother Cat. I nestled in next to my kitten friends.

Mother Cat's milk tasted strange, but it was what I needed. I nursed and felt a little better. Then we all lay together on the square of cloth, Mother Cat and her kittens and me.

After a while, something moved in the light from the hole. I lifted my head. Mother Cat did, too.

I saw a person. A young person. A young male person.

A boy, peering into our home, squinting.

"Kitty? Kitty?"

Mother Cat sniffed the air and climbed to her feet. She left me and the kittens on our piece of cloth. We squirmed a little closer together for warmth and comfort.

"Oh, wow, are you the only one left?" asked the boy. "I don't know what happened. Did somebody take all the other cats while I was at school?"

The boy crawled into the hole. He was different from the people who'd been here before. He didn't shout and grab. He didn't bring blazing lights.

Still, I was wary. This boy could be dangerous. But even though I was frightened of him, I also felt an urge to get up and trot over to him. It was strange, but part of me wanted to be close to a human.

This human.

"They left your bowls, though. Here." Something rattled against metal, and Mother Cat gave a soft meow

of approval. A delicious smell—a food smell—wafted toward me.

"Listen, you can't stay here," the boy said. "They're going to tear down this house, and they're going to do it soon. You'll have to go somewhere safe. I'll figure out what to do. I'm good at figuring stuff out. But you can't stay here much longer, okay?"

The boy crawled back out of the hole, and Mother Cat hurried over to stick her head into the bowl that he had filled with food. After a while, I could not resist. I got up, leaving my kitten friends behind, and went to join her.

Mother Cat did not push me away as my own mother used to do. She let me put my head into the dish beside hers.

Food. Moist, soft food! It was not milk, yet I wanted it in my mouth. It was strange and interesting and delightful, with amazing flavors.

Then I moved on to the other bowl. It felt funny to lap at water instead of sucking in milk, but it also felt right.

Once Mother Cat and I were done, we returned to our piece of cloth. I wondered if the boy would come again.

I hoped so.

The boy did come back, the very next day. He put more food and water in the bowls. Again, I waited with Mother Cat until the boy went away, and

again I followed her and hungrily ate the interesting new food.

The boy came every day. The kittens started coming to the bowls as well, tasting the new food and lapping at the water, just as I did.

Then, once again, everything changed.

Noise came from outside, a new kind of noise that I had never heard before—crunching, grinding, growling. It sounded like something on the other side of the hole was very big and very angry.

Mother Cat was lying on our square of cloth. The kittens had been playing Pounce-and-Jump-Away but now, as the angry noises grew louder and louder, and closer and closer, we looked over at Mother Cat. She stood up, her head turning, her pointed ears alert. The hair along her spine began to lift and bristle.

I knew what that meant. Danger was near.

The kittens and I ran to be near Mother Cat. But being near did not make us feel safer. The noise was so loud that the very ground under our feet was starting to tremble, as if it were afraid, too.

Then the noise became unbearable.

Crash! Above us, something huge had fallen. Our ceiling quaked. Dust rained down in a thick shower. One corner of our den cracked and broke. Light spilled in.

Mother Cat yowled in anger and defiance, turning around and around, her tail lashing the air. But what could she fight? The kittens mewled in terror. I squatted

and peed in the dirt, too scared to keep it in. But none of that made things better.

Through the new hole in our den, I could see what was happening outside. The shapes and colors out there were unfamiliar to my eyes, but I saw something huge that moved across the ground, scraping and crunching at the earth. A growling noise came from deep inside it. That was the threat. I was sure of it.

Then I saw a new shape, something small and quick. It darted in front of the big square object. Dimly, I could hear a sound made by this shape. "Stop! Stop! There are still cats in there!"

It was the voice of the boy, the one who came with food and water. But food and water would not help now.

And the boy could not fight something as huge as that angry, noisy shape. Neither could Mother Cat.

But to my astonishment, the big square loud thing paused and hesitated, as if it were afraid of the boy in front of it.

Another, deeper voice yelled, "Kid, get out of the way!"

"There are cats in there! You can't knock it down! Stop! *Stop!*" the boy shouted.

The big square thing stopped moving. It stopped growling, too. But I was still terrified. Mother Cat's eyes were wide and her ears lay flat against her head. The kittens looked the same.

"What? What are you saying?" called a voice.

"There are cats living in there!" I recognized the boy's voice, but I had no idea what his noises meant.

"No, kid, look, you got it wrong. There were some stray cats in there, sure, but we called some people. They got the cats out. Don't worry. And don't run in front of a bulldozer again! You crazy or something?"

With a snort, the low growl began again. I whimpered, panicked.

"No, they didn't get all of them!" The boy's voice rose. He sounded panicked, too. "There are still cats under the porch. You can't knock the house down now! You'll kill them!"

The growling died away once more. After that there was a lot more of the noises people make with their voices. But at least the growling and crashing did not come back, and the big angry thing did not come any closer. Mother Cat and the kittens and I huddled together on our piece of cloth, all trembling. Mother Cat recovered enough to give us all some licks with her scratchy, strong tongue.

Maybe we were safe now. And maybe the boy would come inside with some food. Food was always good.

But he did not come. Instead, what came inside was light.

Blazing light.

Two people were crawling into our home, carrying the light with them. It was happening again! Whatever had come to take away my brothers and sisters was coming for me!

We all fled the light. I was vaguely aware of Mother Cat diving into the crack in the wall where we had hidden before, while I ran to the new hole in the corner, climbing over dirt and chunks of broken stone.

"Here, kitty, here, kitty," one of the people said, crawling forward. "Can you get that one, Audrey?"

"Got her!"

"Where's the mother?"

I had to get away. I burst out through the hole, landing on the grass.

For the first time in my life, I was outside of the den.

3

The light out here was even brighter than the light the people had carried into the den. And there were so many smells! The grass all around me was taller than I was, and it closed over my head. It smelled alive and sharp.

But there were other smells, too, and lots of those big objects that made the growling noises. They had round wheels and smelled bitter and strange. There were many humans, some standing, some walking with impatient steps, some talking with one another. "Hey, boss, how much longer are we going to wait around?" one of them asked.

It was all bewildering! I did not know what was a threat and what might be safety. My nose was over-whelmed with all the new scents, but I didn't have the luxury of sniffing at them. I had to run!

I pushed through the grass. I didn't know where I was running or what I might find. I just knew that I had to get away.

Then I thumped into something and stopped. I heard a gasp from high above me. It was the boy. "Puppy? Were you living under the house, too?"

I had been in such a blind panic I had blundered right into his legs. He crouched down to see me.

"Puppy, hey, puppy. Come here."

He stretched out a hand toward me.

I did not run anymore. I didn't feel that I *needed* to run. I felt something else entirely.

For reasons I did not understand, I wanted to be close to this boy.

I wanted his hand to touch me. I wanted to hear his voice, for him to talk to me again.

It wasn't just that the boy had been bringing us food. It was far more than that. It seemed right to be near him. To touch him with a paw. To lick his skin and find out what he tasted like.

I wanted this boy.

I bounded forward. He gasped and then laughed. I chewed on his fingers, feeling warm and safe inside, the way I felt when I snuggled with Mother Cat. It was as if all the love in my body was flowing through me, through my jaws, and into the boy.

The boy brought his other hand to me. Carefully, he scooped me up and lifted me close to his chest.

I liked it! I could smell him even better here. I

could burrow inside his jacket and stick my nose into his shirt and sniff up all the smells that I could find. I could lick under his chin.

The boy laughed.

"You're such a silly puppy!" he told me.

I had no idea what his noises meant, but I understood that he was making them at me. I liked that. I licked him again so that he'd make more noises for me.

"Okay, okay, I like you, too," he told me. "Come on."

He stood up, still holding me. Suddenly I was much higher above the ground than I had ever been. New, fresh smells wafted past my nose up here. My heart pounded with excitement and also with joy. I wagged my tail.

I did not know where Mother Cat had gone, nor what had happened to my kitten family. I still missed my first mother and my littermates.

But everything was different now that I had this boy. I somehow knew I was right where I was supposed to be. Everything would be just fine, now.

I heard feet running quickly over the dirt. I pulled my head out from under the boy's chin to see. It was a girl—a young female human.

"Oh!" she said. She had short, dark curly hair, and she was smiling. "I thought for a minute you found another kitten, but it's a puppy! Was she in the crawl-space, too?"

"I think so," the boy said. "Anyway, she doesn't have a collar."

I decided to go back to licking the boy's face.

"Aw, she likes you," the girl said.

She reached out a hand and rubbed behind my ears. That felt good. I liked this girl, too.

"You're Lucas, right? I'm Olivia. You stopped that bulldozer! That's amazing! Everybody's talking about it. Here, give the puppy to me. I'll take her to my mom. She works at the rescue."

"Um," the boy said.

"You want to take her to the car? We've got a crate she can go in."

I cuddled close to the boy and chewed contentedly on his fingers.

"I don't want to take her to the car, no."

The boy and the girl looked at each other for a few moments while I enjoyed the boy's fingers.

"Okay, what?" said the girl.

"I thought I'd just take her home," the boy said.

"Oh! Well, look, we're not really supposed to do that. You can't just grab a stray puppy. There's a whole process to adopting a dog. Forms and stuff. And my mom has to interview the people. We want to be sure they're going to good homes. You know?"

"You think I'm not going to take good care of her?" the boy asked.

The girl sighed. "Of course you are. I mean, you saved her life! And she loves you. That's pretty obvious. I just . . . okay. My mom's coming over. Put the puppy in your jacket and cover her up, okay? And don't tell my mom!"

The boy carefully tucked me inside his coat. He held one arm under me, to keep me safe. I felt as cozy as I did while snuggling with my dog mother and my littermates, or my cat mother and her kittens.

I could feel the boy's heart pounding close to his skin. He was happy and excited, too, just as I was. He was as glad to be with me as I was to be with him. But he was worried about something. What? Wasn't everything okay now?

"Hello, are you Lucas?" a woman's voice said. "I have to thank you for insisting they stop tearing down the house. The cats would have been injured or killed for certain. And did you hear that one of the workers saw a puppy?"

I felt the boy's body snap to attention. "No, ma'am, no one told me that. The workers were kind of angry at me."

"I imagine so! The manager told me they lost a day's work," the woman replied.

"Mom, Lucas ran right out in front of a bulldozer and started shouting and waving his arms!" the girl exclaimed.

"Did you get the cats?" the boy asked.

"We caught all the kittens," the woman said. "The mom escaped, but we'll keep looking for her. We'll find homes for the kittens. I wonder, though, where that puppy went?"

"I think somebody found it and wants to give it a good home," the girl suggested.

I was starting to squirm a little inside the boy's jacket.

I had to pee. And I always peed on the ground, not up in the air under a jacket like this.

"Hey, lady, can we get going on this job?" a man's voice called. "I've got guys on the clock here."

"Go ahead," the woman said. "We checked in the crawlspace. No more cats or dogs or—Lucas, wait a minute. What's that in your jacket?"

The boy froze.

"What do you mean?" the boy replied.

"It looks like you're carrying a baseball mitt," the woman observed.

"I often do," the boy agreed.

"Interesting answer, Lucas."

The boy was Lucas, I decided.

I heard a man shouting, "Let's get back to work!"

Then the angry growling started up again with a roar. I twitched, startled, and struggled to get out of the jacket.

There was a long pause.

"Better get home," the woman said. "I don't think your baseball mitt likes the noise of the bulldozer. And you've got to take it to a vet as soon as you can."

"Uh. Yeah. Okay," Lucas mumbled. "Thanks." And he started walking away quickly, holding me tightly to him all the while. I popped my head up and looked around in amazement.

Something was happening to me here. The den, where I had been born and where I'd lived with Mother

Cat, seemed like a place that I was leaving behind. Now I would be with this boy, wherever he took me.

The boy walked for a while, holding me close, and then he stopped. I felt him sit down. He took me out of his jacket and set me on the ground. That was a relief. I squatted and peed right away.

"Good boy!" the boy said to me. "Um, good girl, I mean."

I looked around and sniffed to see where he had taken me.

He was sitting on a single step outside of a large building. At the top of the step there was a door. I looked around. There were other steps and other doors along this side of the building.

Later I would learn that, just like Lucas lived behind his door, other people lived behind the other doors. Some of them even had dogs or cats of their own.

For now, I was busy checking out what was right in front of me. On either side of the steps there were bushes, and some dogs had been here before me, peeing on them. I very carefully examined these important scents.

The boy laughed. I left the bushes and ran to him and seized the cuff of his pants between my front teeth. I tugged on it.

Lucas laughed again. But he was not entirely happy. I could hear it in his voice. I could see it in the angle of his head and shoulders.

I sat back on my haunches and looked up at him. Why wasn't he as happy as I was?

"I didn't really think this through," he told me. "I could be in pretty big trouble."

I cocked my head up at him. Could he be talking about food? I liked food.

"My mom . . . I don't know. She might be pretty unhappy. But you and I belong together, little pup."

The boy sighed. He picked me up again.

"Okay, let's go," he said.

He carried me up to the door, opened it, and went inside.

4

Once we stepped inside, there were so many new sounds and sights that I was dizzy with it. And the smells! I could smell food and dust and chemicals and a woman.

The boy set me down, and the floor was astonishingly soft beneath my feet—even softer than the dirt in my old den. I ran after him as he crossed the room and dove into his lap when he sat down on the floor to be with me.

I could sense his anxiety rising. What was he worried about?

"Lucas?" called a sleepy voice. "What's that?"

The voice came from the woman whose scent was layered on every object in the room. Clearly this was her den, and the boy's, too.

She was lying on a long, soft thing that I later

learned was called a couch. A blanket was covering her so that only her head and shoulders showed. She was stretching as if she'd just woken up, though her arms were in the air and not out in front of her on the floor. I wagged, happy to see her.

"Lucas?" she said again.

Lucas looked up at her.

"It's a puppy," he said.

"Well, I can see it's a puppy, Lucas. What is it doing here?"

"She's a girl. Not an *it*."

"That is not an answer to my question."

"She was living in the house across the street," Lucas explained, cuddling me in both hands. "The one where the stray cats were. The cats I was feeding. The animal rescue people came and got the cats, and I found this little girl, all lost and confused and alone and needing a good home like ours."

He put me on the floor and I hurried over to the couch. The woman wasn't the boy, but I wanted to get to know her.

She put a hand over the edge of the couch and I jumped up to sniff it. She smelled tired and in pain. I licked her to show that I'd help her. I'd comfort her, if she wanted me to.

"And you brought her to *our* home because . . ." the woman said.

"Because look at her. Someone abandoned her and she found her way under that house. She was living

there with the cats. And she was so scared of the bull-dozer. She ran right to me."

"Right. I understand. But, Lucas—"

"She ran to me. She's my dog now."

"Lucas, you know we can't have a dog. Do you have any idea how expensive it would be? Vet bills and dog food, it adds up pretty quickly."

"I'll get a job. I'll earn some money."

"Lucas. Listen. You don't have time for that. Once the summer is over, you've got to focus on school. You're only thirteen, and—"

"Focus on school? I do focus on school! Are you saying there is a problem with my grades?"

Lucas scooted forward so he could pet me, too. Now both humans were touching me! I wagged my tail so hard my entire back end wiggled.

"You're trying to make this about something else. Obviously I don't have a problem with your grades, Lucas. You do so well in school. You're doing so well around here, too. I know I'm not much help."

"I can take care of things," Lucas insisted. "Until you get better."

"I know you can. You already are. You clean up the apartment, you do the shopping, you cook half the time. And now a dog, too? Lucas, it's too much."

"Don't I get to decide if it's too much?"

There was a long silence. I looked back and forth from the boy to the woman. I wagged hopefully. I barked a tiny bark. When were they going to stop looking at

each other and play with me? Wasn't that why we were all here?

"If I keep my grades up and help around here and get a job to make some money, can I keep her?" the boy asked. "If I do all that?"

The woman sighed.

"You shouldn't have to do all that, Lucas. I'm so sorry . . ."

"You don't have to be sorry you got hurt. It was a war, Mom. Soldiers get hurt in wars. I know that." Lucas pulled me into his lap once more. Finally! I set about chewing his fingers. "But you're home from Afghanistan now, and I'm taking care of you," he said.

The woman's head flopped back onto the pillow. "Oh, honey," she said.

"And I can take care of a dog, too. Please, Mom? Please?"

The woman's head lifted off the pillow. I stopped nibbling on Lucas and stared at her. "The way you two are looking at me, how can I say no?" she asked.

Over the next several days, I slowly became used to living in my new home. It was not like the den at all. The surface underfoot was not dirt. Instead, I ran on hard, slippery floors or soft carpeted ones. Light streamed in through many windows and glowed from globes in the ceiling. There were no cats or other dogs anywhere, but there were people. Two people. My people.

The woman's name, I learned, was Mom. She was nice.

Lucas! I loved Lucas so much. I followed him from room to room. I sat on his feet when he was in a chair or the couch. Sometimes I took his fingers in my mouth. I didn't bite down. I just nibbled him as gently as I could. I loved the taste and the nearness of his skin.

I slept next to him in a soft pile of blankets that I shredded a little until I came to understand how unhappy this made him. I did not want Lucas to be unhappy at all.

I pulled one of those blankets onto the floor so I could snuggle up in it whenever I wanted. It smelled like Lucas, which made me happy. Curling up in it while Lucas was busy was nearly as good as lying next to him in bed. I thought of it as my Lucas blanket.

Lucas was busy a lot. He opened and shut cupboards in the kitchen. This activity often went along with delicious smells. He stood at the sink and splashed his hands in soapy water. Sometimes he pulled out a long stick with bristles on the end of it and rubbed it on the floor. I helped by chasing the bristles and biting them.

When Lucas was not busy with his jobs—and even when he was—he talked to me. A lot.

"Quiet, Bella, we can't make noise. Mom's sleeping," he'd tell me.

"Here, Bella, I've got a toy for you! Bella, come!"

"Want a treat, Bella? Treat?"

Whenever he said this, I gazed up at him. I felt that he expected me to do something, but I didn't know what.

Then he'd pull his hand out of his pocket and give me a tiny chunk of something crunchy and meaty. The taste of it would flood my tongue.

Treat! Soon it was my favorite word.

And that other word that Lucas used so often—it became a favorite as well. *Bella*. Over and over, Lucas said, "Bella!" and I came to realize that when he said it, he meant me.

Bella was my name.

Lucas introduced me to all sorts of wonderful tastes and experiences, but one of my favorites came when he was sitting at his desk and I could smell something so insanely delicious my tongue was going berserk. I was licking my lips, staring up at him, whimpering. He smiled down at me. "You want some cheese, Bella?"

I heard the question in his voice and wagged frantically.

"Okay, just a tiny bit. Okay, here you go, a T-i-i-ny Piece of Cheese."

He held out a finger, and on it was a sliver of something so delicious it nearly made me swoon.

After that day, every night, Lucas would say, "Bella, are you ready for your T-i-i-ny Piece of Cheese?"

I would sit, quivering, waiting impatiently for the magnificent T-i-i-ny Piece of Cheese.

Several times a day, Lucas would bring out some-

thing he called *the leash,* and snap it onto a thing around my neck, which he called *your collar.* He used the leash to drag me around. At first, I hated the thing because it made no sense to me. Why was Lucas pulling me in one direction when there were so many exciting smells in the other?

But then I learned that, when Lucas had the leash, we were going outside for what he called *a walk.* And I loved a walk! A walk meant fascinating smells, and new people who petted me and laughed at me and seemed so happy to see me.

One new person who came over often was named Olivia. She was the girl who had talked to Lucas on the day he became my boy.

Olivia liked to take walks with us. And she liked to play games with us. She knew a lot of games. "I'm going to be a dog trainer," she told Lucas. "Bella's going to be a big dog when she grows up—you can tell—so you better start training her now, when she's still a puppy."

Here are some of the games Lucas and I played with Olivia.

"Sit!" meant that I'd put my rear end on the ground and get a treat.

"Down!" meant I'd put my belly on the ground and get another treat.

Sometimes Olivia would hold my leash while Lucas walked away. Then he would call, "Come!" and she'd let me go. I'd run and run and run to Lucas and get another treat.

Olivia understood how much dogs like treats. I liked Olivia.

One game that we played, however, was not my favorite. It was called Do-Your-Business.

"Do your business!" Lucas or Olivia would say while we walked. Then sometimes one of them would give me a treat. Sometimes they wouldn't.

Very strange and a bit frustrating. It was much more fun to go a place they called *the park*. I loved the park. There was a big grassy meadow where I could be off the leash. Lucas and Olivia would bring a ball with them and they'd throw it for me so that I could chase it and catch it and bring it back so they could do it again. That ball never got away from me.

Chase-the-Ball didn't even need treats to be an excellent game.

Once Lucas threw the ball extra hard, and it flew over to a place where children sometimes played on swings. I was right behind it, gaining fast, when it bounced onto a plastic ramp and rolled to the top.

I followed, trying to grip the slippery surface. At the top of the ramp the ball kept going and so did I. I jumped off and caught the ball in the air after it hit the ground.

"Bella!" Lucas called. "You ran up the slide! Good dog, Bella!"

After that we played Chase-the-Ball-Up-the-Slide a lot. And then we'd head home.

I loved our home. Mom would be there and I would

run to her for hugs. Sometimes she was lying on the couch and sometimes sitting in a chair and sometimes walking around, leaning on a special stick that I learned early on not to chew.

If she was sitting, I'd put my front feet up on her lap so she could pet me properly, and she would laugh and tell me, "Down!" but I knew she wanted to pet me as much as I wanted to be petted, so it didn't matter what she said.

I loved when Lucas put food in my bowl. I loved when he held me on his lap. I loved *him*. My world had Lucas at its center. If my eyes were open, they were looking for him. If my nose was twitching, it was searching for him.

Every day brought new joys, new things to do with Lucas.

"Bella, you are the best little puppy in the world," he told me, kissing me.

I was Bella, and Lucas was my person. We were together, and that was perfect.

And then something horrible happened.

5

One day Lucas knelt down on the floor and put one hand on either side of my face, looking right into my eyes. "I'll be back, Bella. I have to go to school, but you know I'll be back."

And then he left, shutting the door behind him. He was gone for so long I thought he had forgotten me. I thought I would never see him again. I sprawled on the floor in front of the door so if he came back I could greet him immediately.

"He'll be home soon, I promise, Bella," Mom told me. I heard my name but didn't wag my tail.

Then, finally, at long, long last, Lucas came home! I went berserk, running around the room, jumping on and off furniture, squirming and wagging and yipping and licking his face while he laughed at me. I was so happy *that* was over with!

But then, the next morning, the exact same thing happened.

And the day after that!

It was impossible to believe, but apparently this was going to be how my mornings were going to go, now.

"Okay, Bella," Lucas would say. "I have to go to school now."

I'd whine and squirm a little bit, because when he talked to me like that, I knew what was coming.

Lucas would stand up, walk quickly to the door, open it, and go outside. Then he'd shut the door behind him. I would be inside, and Lucas would be outside!

This was terrible.

I'd cry. I'd pace back and forth in front of the door.

"Bella," Mom would say from the couch. "Bella, it's okay. Come here, Bella."

I'd go to Mom and sit beside her for a little while. She was not Lucas, but she did okay at stroking my head and scratching my ears. It was a little comforting.

"I miss him, too," Mom would tell me. "He'll be back."

I knew I had to wait for Lucas. I would wait and wait as hard as I could.

And then I would bark. If I barked loudly enough and long enough, Lucas would hear me and come home. I knew it.

"Bella!" Mom would say over the noise I was making. "Bella, stop. Please. Bella, no more barking!"

I wondered what she was making noise about. Maybe

she was barking in a human way, so that Lucas would come back soon. We both needed Lucas to come home and show that he still loved us and would never leave again.

The barking always worked. Lucas always came home. I'd fling myself at his feet, frantically happy. I'd bite at his pants and jump up on his legs until he sat down to pull me into his lap. I'd lick his chin and push my face into his hair, so happy to be with my person again that I almost forgot how horrible it was when he was gone.

Lucas usually took me for a walk as soon as he got home, which made our reunions even more wonderful. I figured out as we went on these walks that Do-Your-Business had to do with peeing and pooping. If Lucas said those words and I left a puddle or a pile on the ground, I got a treat.

It still wasn't as good as Chase-the-Ball, but it seemed to make Lucas happy.

Even better than Chase-the-Ball was another game, one I figured out all by myself. It was called Chase-the-Squirrel.

Lucas and I were heading back home after a nice long walk full of delightful smells when I spotted a tiny, furry creature sniffing the grass near our front door. Immediately my whole body stiffened. My nose tracked the little thing. It was running! It needed to be chased!

I chased it. The leash slipped out of Lucas's hand, which made the game even better. I could put all my

energy into my legs, and I shot across a lawn with my tail thrashing the air. I'd get the squirrel!

But the little furry thing was even faster than I was. It streaked across the grass to a nearby tree—and then it did an astonishing thing. It ran *up* the tree!

How unfair! I could not run up the tree. Instead, I danced around under the branches, and then put my front legs on the trunk and barked as loudly as I could, frustrated. I looked frantically at Lucas. If he would just help me up the tree, I could get that squirrel! I knew it!

Lucas came panting up, but for some reason he did not boost me up to the squirrel. He just grabbed the leash and took me home.

That was okay. I knew where that squirrel lived, now.

One morning when Lucas took me outside, the ground was different! It was covered in something fluffy and white that felt extremely cold on my paws.

I stared in astonishment. I looked up at Lucas. What was this new white stuff? Had he put it there?

"It's just snow, Bella!" he told me. "Just snow. Do your business!"

I peered suspiciously at the Snow Do Your Business.

Holding the leash, Lucas ran a little way out into the cold whiteness. "Come on! It's fun!"

I ran with him, because he was my boy. The white fluff flew up all around me. I stuck my head into it. I

snorted when it got into my nose. I bit at it. It tasted cold and watery. Lucas laughed, so I pulled my head out of the snow and gazed at him adoringly.

I decided I *loved* Snow Do Your Business!

Sometimes the ground was covered with Snow Do Your Business, and some days it wasn't. Either way we would go to the park and I would run up the slide. The world grew warmer and greener, and Lucas and Olivia and I took walks and chased balls and squirrels, and everything was marvelous, except when Lucas went away and I had to bark to make him come back.

Then something truly marvelous happened. It was called *summer.*

Summer meant Lucas stopped going away. He stayed home! At last he had figured out that he was not supposed to leave me. I didn't know why it had taken him so long—I had always known that we should be together all day long.

And we were, for so many long, wonderful days. Until the day that Lucas, for some reason, started talking about school again.

I did not know what school was. But I did not like it. When Lucas said *school,* he left. And every so often, Mom left, too! She would go out the door, leaning on her stick, and be gone a long time! When this happened, all the responsibility of barking and barking would fall on me.

It was a lot of work. But I did it for Lucas.

Lucas always paid attention to my barking and came

back home. It just took him such a long time! One day after he'd finally returned and greeted me and petted me and put on my leash, we went out for our walk. I was playing Chase-the-Squirrel, and Lucas was playing Chase-the-Dog, when someone shouted.

"That's the dog!" the person cried out. "Get him!"

The squirrel that I was chasing had gone up a tree *again*. And Lucas still hadn't figured out that he was supposed to help me when that happened! While I was barking at that irritating squirrel, Lucas came up to grab my leash and tug me away.

I wasn't finished playing, but I went with him.

"Hey, kid," a man said. He was dressed in dark clothes and wore a hat. I wagged at him as he approached, because he carried the odor of dogs on him. Behind him was a woman who was frowning. I wagged at her because I could smell cats.

"Yes, Officer?" Lucas replied.

The man and the woman stopped. I strained to go see them and lick their hands, but Lucas held me back.

"You know you're not supposed to let your dog run loose," the man said sternly.

"Sorry," Lucas answered. "She loves to chase the squirrels so much, I just dropped the leash to let her go. I won't do it again."

"What kind of dog is it?" the man asked.

The woman pointed her finger. "It's a pit bull! He let a dangerous pit bull run around in the neighborhood. He does it all the time! A child could have been killed!"

Whatever we were doing seemed like it was going to take some time, so I flopped down on the ground and rolled on my back, because if they were just going to stand around the least they could do was take turns giving me a belly rub.

"Ma'am, thank you for calling animal control. I can handle it from here," the man in the hat said to the woman, his voice heavy with patience.

"I'm telling you, you have to arrest this dog!" the woman cried.

The hat man sighed.

"I guess she's a pit bull," Lucas said. "I mean, she doesn't *look* like it, but I was told her mother was a white pit bull. Maybe that's why Bella has this white star on her chest."

Lucas leaned down and rubbed my chest and tummy. Yes!

"They were bred to be killers. I have cats who are outside all the time and this dog is a danger to all of them! If you don't do your job I am going to call your supervisor!" the woman said harshly.

Hat Man regarded the woman with narrowed eyes. "So you let your cats run free? Do you know that's against the law?"

The woman's mouth dropped open.

Hat Man peered down the street. "Are your cats out now?"

"Well. I've done my duty and reported the animal,"

the woman said curtly. She turned and walked away—no belly rub from her.

Hat Man knelt next to me and *yes*, ran his hand gently down my chest and stomach. "Doesn't seem very dangerous to me," he remarked.

"Bella's the most gentle dog you can imagine," Lucas replied.

The man nodded and sighed again. "I'm really sorry you told me she's a pit bull. Especially in front of a witness. Especially *that* witness."

"What do you mean?" Lucas asked.

"Pit bulls are illegal within city limits. We can't come on your property without your permission, but you're not on your property—you're on the sidewalk. I'm sorry to say I'm going to have to take Bella with me now." Hat Man stood up.

"Wait! What? Take her, what do you mean?" Lucas cried. I got to my feet, wagging, confused and worried. My boy was upset!

"I have to impound her. It's my job, son. I'm sorry."

"No. Please. I'll never let her run loose again, I promise!" Lucas begged. I put a paw on his leg because he was so sad and frightened.

"I wish it were that simple, kid. That lady has called our office probably a dozen times to report you, because you can't even have a pit bull on a leash here. Understand? Not on the street, not in the dog park, nowhere but your own property."

"Please, Officer, please don't take my dog."

Hat Man was quiet. Then he leaned in. "Okay, look. We pretty much ignore that woman, because she calls and says every dog is a pit bull. Rottweilers, bull dogs, you name it. Yours, though, you said it was a pit bull. That's a different story."

"No, I mean, we could do a DNA test or something . . ." Lucas protested.

Hat Man shook his head. "That won't work. It isn't about DNA, it is about what people think they see. Perception, understand? It's too late; she heard you say pit bull. So, and you didn't hear this from me, don't ever let that woman see your dog again. Understand? I'm going to let you go, but if I see Bella again, I'm going to have to pick her up. I don't want to get written up by my commanding officer."

"I mean, we live right over there," Lucas replied. He pointed and I looked, but didn't see any squirrels. "How can I stop her from seeing us?"

Hat Man shrugged. "I don't know. I get that you have to take your dog outside sometimes. And remember, I'm not allowed to enter your apartment or even go on your porch. But this is your one and only warning. You want Bella to be safe? You should find someone who doesn't live in city limits, and give her away."

Lucas gasped.

"I'm just saying, that's what I would do," Hat Man said.

6

Lucas walked me back home. I was happy to see Mom, but Lucas was sad, so I curled up at his feet when he sat in a chair to talk to her.

"Oh, Lucas," Mom said, "that is such bad news. What are we going to do?"

"We have to move, Mom!" Lucas replied forcefully. "We need to go where they allow pit bulls!"

"I know there are neighborhoods nearby that are pit bull friendly," Mom said slowly, "but, Lucas, we can't just move. We have a lease."

"What does that mean?" Lucas asked.

"A lease is a contract I signed to rent our place for a year. If we move before a year is up, we have to pay a big penalty. It's more money than I have, Lucas."

"A year? Mom, we can't keep Bella inside our home for a year. I have to walk her so she can do her business."

I sat up. Walk? Snow Do Your Business? There hadn't been any Snow Do Your Business on the ground for some time, but maybe things had changed.

"I know, Lucas, but what else can we do? I'll tell you what," Mom replied. "Doesn't Olivia's mother work for an animal rescue? Let's ask them to come over and see if they have any ideas."

Lucas was upset, I could tell, but thankfully not so upset that he forgot T-i-i-ny Piece of Cheese that night. It was one of the most important things we did together.

The next day, Lucas and I were playing in the bedroom. He pulled a string along the floor. I jumped on it and ran away with it, but it slipped out of my mouth, and he laughed and pulled it along the floor until I could pounce again.

I was so happy to be with him, to hear his laughter, that I could have played that game all day.

Then somebody rang the doorbell. My ears perked up. Whenever the doorbell rang, it was one of my jobs to bark a loud warning that a stranger was here. Sometimes Lucas and Mom would join their voices to mine, shouting their own warnings. "Stop it!" they'd yell. "Quiet!"

It was one of my favorite jobs.

I was overjoyed to see who it was. Olivia! Plus a woman I had a vague memory of smelling before. Olivia was confused and called this new person Mom, which was strange. Mom called her Audrey, so that's what I decided her name was.

At first all the people sat in the living room and

BORDERS®

Merchandise presented for return, including sale or marked-down items, must be accompanied by the original Borders store receipt. Returns must be completed within 30 days of purchase. The purchase price will be refunded in the medium of purchase (cash, credit card or gift card). Items purchased by check may be returned for cash after 10 business days.

Merchandise unaccompanied by the original Borders store receipt, or presented for return beyond 30 days from date of purchase, must be carried by Borders at the time of the return. The lowest price offered for the item during the 12 month period prior to the return will be refunded via a gift card.

Opened videos, discs, and cassettes may only be exchanged for replacement copies of the original item.
Periodicals, newspapers, out-of-print, collectible and pre-owned items may not be returned.
Returned merchandise must be in saleable condition.

BORDERS®

BORDERS

BORDERS
BOOKS MUSIC AND CAFE
100 Broadway
New York, NY 10005
(212)964-1988

STORE: 0566   REG: 08/68 TRAN#: 4479
SALE   12/27/2004 EMP: 00122

STUPIDEST ANGEL
     7566894   CL T   14.95

       Subtotal   14.95
       NEW YORK 8.625% 1.28
1 Item   Total   16.23
       GIFT CARD   16.23
ACCT # /S XXXXXXXXXXXX2092
        AUTH: 649673
ACCOUNT BALANCE:8.77

12/27/2004 12:37PM

Check our store inventory online
at www.bordersstores.com

Shop online at www.borders.com

talked. Mom and Audrey sipped hot drinks out of mugs and they ate cookies off a plate, but nobody offered any to me.

"We've been trying to fight this law for years," Audrey said. "If Bella gets taken to a shelter once, they'll microchip her. If she gets picked up a second time, I'm afraid they'll put her to sleep."

Lucas gasped. I went over and put my head in his lap so that he'd remember everything was okay, and also that I hadn't had a cookie yet.

"That's so unfair!" Olivia said angrily.

"I know, honey," Audrey replied. "It's strange, because you're not breaking the law by *keeping* Bella. You're only in trouble if they *catch* Bella. Which means the most important thing is to keep Bella out of sight— and sound. I heard her when we rang your doorbell. Does she always bark like that?"

"Oh, yes," Lucas replied ruefully.

"She also barks when Lucas leaves for school," Mom added.

Lucas put his arms around my neck and his face on my head. I wagged.

"Well, that's something we can deal with," Audrey said.

That was when we started to play a new game. It was called No Barks.

I did not like this game.

First Olivia went outside and shut the door. Then she rang the doorbell.

I knew it was my job to bark at the doorbell. But Lucas sat down next to me in the hallway and put his whole hand over my snout. "No Barks!" he said firmly.

We did that several times, even though it was no fun at all. It was as if Lucas didn't want me to do my job! What was going on?

The doorbell rang again, and Lucas clamped his hand around my muzzle. I sat down on the floor and stared at him in bewilderment. "Good dog, Bella!" Lucas said. He took his hand off my muzzle and gave me a treat.

I began to like this game a little better.

Then Lucas went outside and rang the doorbell, which was very odd. He never did that! Each time, Olivia or Mom told me, "No Barks," and I realized that if I was quiet, I would be a good dog who got treats. I even tried it when the bell rang and no one said anything to me. Treats! I decided right then that it was better to let the doorbell ring without making any sort of announcement than to do what I had always considered to be one of my most important jobs.

"Our next problem is harder," Audrey said. "You can't keep a dog cooped up inside all day, especially one as young as Bella."

Hearing my name, I looked at her eagerly. There had been a lot of treats today, and I was hoping that would continue.

"The animal control officer told me if he saw me walking her, he would have to pick her up," Lucas pointed out.

"Right. But he also said he won't come up on your porch to take her," Audrey replied. "And that's something I think we can work with."

I was really excited when Lucas brought out the leash. "Hold still, you silly dog!" he told me.

"Where does that lady live?" Olivia asked.

Lucas went to the window and I followed. "Right down there in that white house," he replied.

"Okay. I'll go check to see if she's in her yard or looking out the window," Olivia said. She slipped out the door.

I watched her go, baffled. Didn't she know we were about to take a walk? Why would she leave now? She must never have seen a squirrel before. I sat tensely, staring up at my boy, who was still staring out the window. "Okay," he said to Mom and Audrey. "She's waving."

"Good luck," Mom said.

Lucas and I left, practically running until we were down the street and around the corner. Then he stopped. I sat, not sure what we were doing. Then Olivia came! She wanted to go for a walk after all!

"Her car isn't there. We can do this," Oliva said.

"Okay, Bella. Time for you to learn how to go home," Lucas said, his hand rustling in his pocket. I stared because I could smell treats in there.

Then, in a move that was even more bewildering, Lucas left me with Olivia. I watched, utterly perplexed, as he walked down the street and up the steps to our home.

"Go Home!" Olivia told me. She dropped the leash.

"Here, Bella!" Lucas called.

I ran straight to Lucas. Lucas knelt down beside the door and patted a spot behind a chair. His hand smelled very interesting—he had one of those treats in there!

I nosed at his hand, but he just kept patting. Then I remembered that Lucas often wanted me to lie down somewhere if he patted it. I flopped down and got the treat. Excellent!

We played Go Home a lot. At first I ran straight to Lucas and lay down by the door and got my treat. Then Lucas picked up my leash and we walked together with Olivia by our side. Maybe we were going to the park. That would be fun.

Then Lucas dropped my leash. "Go Home!" he told me.

I stared up at him. This was very odd. Go Home meant running to Lucas! But Lucas was already here!

Lucas and Olivia were watching me intently.

"She'll get it," Olivia said to Lucas. "She's really smart. Just wait."

They stared at me. I stared at them. They wanted me to do something. But what?

They wanted me to do Go Home. Go Home meant running to Lucas and lying down by the chair and getting a treat.

But Lucas was right next to me. I could not run to Lucas.

I could lie down. I did that. I looked up hopefully.

"She doesn't get it," Lucas said to Olivia. He sounded unhappy.

I was frustrated. Where was my treat? I was lying down. When I lay down before, Lucas gave me a treat.

But I hadn't been lying down on the sidewalk. I'd been lying down behind the chair, next to the door. Was that what Lucas wanted?

Why?

The treats in his pocket were my favorite—chicken—and that's what made me decide to take a chance. I sprang up and raced toward the door. Once I got there, I lay down behind the chair, just like I'd done before.

Would I get a treat *now*?

"Bella! Good girl!" Lucas shouted. He and Olivia came running up, and he gave me *two* treats. "That was amazing!" he told me.

He and Olivia were so happy that we played the Go Home game over and over. I liked it very much. Go Home meant running and treats and a happy Lucas.

I loved Lucas.

After that day with Olivia, we played Go Home often on our walks. Lucas would unsnap my leash, and I would run back to our house and curl up beside the door. When we did Go Home, I was a good dog who was given food. But somehow, when we played No Barks, I never felt like a good dog, even when I got a treat.

"She's so smart," Lucas told Mom. "I told her to go home all the way from the park, and even though she wanted to go in and play with the other dogs, she turned right around and came here and was waiting behind the chair for me when I got back."

"Good dog, Bella," Mom praised. I wagged.

"So now, even if animal control sees me with her, I can just take the leash off and give her the command, and she'll run up on the porch where she is safe."

"Are you positive it will work?" Mom asked.

Lucas was silent for a long moment. "It has to, Mom. I don't know what else to do."

7

The next day, Lucas said *school* and went away. Mom did, too, leaning on her stick. I did No Barks, but nobody was there to give me treats. Sighing, I went into the kitchen and nosed open a door to a small room where my food was kept in a bag on a shelf, up out of reach. I kept hoping one day I would open the door and the bag would be lying on the floor, but so far that hadn't happened.

When Mom walked in the door I was excited to see her. But something unusual was going on: Mom paced in the living room, pausing to peer out the window. She also picked up her phone and stared at it. A phone is something people will look at and talk to like it is a dog. I guess Mom and Lucas had gotten into the habit of doing this before I got there. They must have been crazy with loneliness without a dog.

"He'll be here in a few minutes, Bella!" Mom said to me. I wagged at her excitement.

When Lucas walked in the door, Mom and I both tried to get to him first. I put my legs up on him while Mom reached around me for a hug. "Lucas, I got a job!"

Lucas stared at her. I decided his arrival called for a ball and raced to get one.

"I thought you said you didn't feel ready for that yet," Lucas was saying when I returned. I dropped the ball at his feet and gazed at it suggestively, waiting for him to get it and throw it. We really needed a slide in the living room, I decided.

"It's perfect because I will be working in Dr. Gann's department at the VA," Mom said enthusiastically, "so I'll actually have more support than what I can get here at home. It's just part time. And you know what this means, don't you?"

"I just don't want you pushing yourself too hard," Lucas replied.

"Lucas, the extra income means we'll have the money to break our lease and move! We can be in a new place in two months!" Mom said happily.

"You would do that for me?" Lucas whispered. I abandoned the ball because I felt a rush of emotion in Lucas, like heat on his skin. Not sadness, but something.

"Not for you, for us. For our family!" Mom beamed.

That night we took a long walk. For some time, it

seemed like Lucas liked the darkness. We only headed outside before the sun brightened the sky in the morning, or after it had vanished in the evening. I didn't mind—there were just as many interesting smells in darkness as in light.

"It's going to be okay, Bella," Lucas told me. "I thought we were going to have to do this for ten more months, but now it will be less than two. You're safe!"

Whatever he was saying, I could tell he was happy. I was, too.

I noticed a change, though—now, when Lucas said *school* and left, Mom would tell me *work* and she would leave as well. I could manage life alone, but it seemed to be happening every day.

Whatever work was, it seemed to make Mom happy. "Thank you, Bella," she whispered to me once. "Thank you for forcing me to quit making excuses. I thought it would be too hard for me, but I love having a purpose in the world beyond just healing myself. You gave me that. I love you."

I wagged at Mom's hugs, but then she left and I was alone once more.

This new set of circumstances left me bored. My legs ached to run. I wandered the apartment. Usually I curled up and slept on my Lucas blanket until my boy got home again, but I didn't feel like doing that right now. Too many days had passed where all I could do was nap and wait.

After a while of pacing, I stood by a window. The

glass part of the window had been moved up, and only the screen was left between me and all the good smells coming in from outside. Trash. Leaves. People walking past. The burned, bitter smell that cars left when they drove by. Squirrel.

Squirrel!

My ears perked up. My body tensed. There it was—I could see it as well as smell it. A small, furry body was scampering across the grass not ten feet away from me.

It was time to play Chase-the-Squirrel!

Before I even had time to think about it, I coiled my back legs and surged forward in a powerful leap. My head crashed into the screen, but the screen could not hold me back. It gave way with a sound like cloth tearing, only louder, and I was through the window, all four feet landing on the lawn.

The screen was still clinging to my neck like a strange, prickly collar, but it wasn't slowing me down. I lunged toward the squirrel, and it streaked across the lawn, heading for a tree.

This time it wouldn't get away. I'd catch it for sure!

I got so close to the squirrel I could almost taste its tail, but in the end it whisked up a tree as they always do, leaving me to stand on my hind legs with my front feet up on the trunk and bark and bark and bark.

When I tired of trying to coax the squirrel out of the tree, I left and started sniffing the bushes. Some male dogs had been there before me.

"Oh, no," said a new voice.

I turned my head and there was Hat Man! He still had the hat on, and he smelled the same, of sweat and smoke and the scent of lots and lots of dogs. He was standing a very short distance from me. "What are you doing out here?"

He knelt and I went to him, wagging my tail. He reached out and pulled off the screen—I was glad to get rid of that collar! I licked his hand and he sighed. "Now what am I supposed to do?" he whispered to me.

I looked over his shoulder and wagged because the woman who smelled like cats was coming toward us rapidly. "I told you!" she called as she approached. "I see them walking that animal all the time! Why haven't you come when I called?"

"I did come, ma'am. I'm here, aren't I?" Hat Man reached into his pocket and took something out. A treat! I gobbled it up, glad to know this new friend.

Somehow, while I was eating the treat, Hat Man slipped a strange new collar over my head. And suddenly I was on the worst leash imaginable—stiff and hard, like a branch from a tree. I twisted against it. "No!" Hat Man said curtly.

I stared up at him astonishment. No? Why was he saying no? Anyone would want to get this leash off!

"That dog needs to be destroyed before it bites somebody else!" the woman declared hotly.

"Oh? Who did she bite?" Hat Man asked.

I sat, thinking if I was good the bad leash would be removed from my neck.

"It's a lucky thing no child was injured," the woman replied. I decided I didn't like anything about her except how she smelled.

"You do know you're more likely to be bitten by a Chihuahua than this dog?" Hat Man asked.

"You should be glad I called you," the woman replied.

"Yes, thank you," Hat Man said. He dragged me over to the street! I did not like it. This was not like going for a walk—it was something else. It was scary.

I whined and pulled and tried to look around for Lucas. Where was he?

A small truck was parked by the curb. It smelled of gas and metal and smoke, the way all cars do, but it also smelled of dogs. Unhappy dogs. A loud, shrill yapping was coming from inside it.

Hat Man opened a door on the back of the truck and then grabbed me with one arm, holding the stiff leash with the other. He lifted me up. I didn't like having my feet in the air. I barked sharply.

The man dropped me inside the truck and pushed me into a crate. Then he pulled the new collar off over my head. I shook my head. The door to the crate slammed shut.

Next to my crate was another with a small dog inside. Once I was nearby, this little dog stopped yapping and cowered away.

Hat Man closed the door to the truck. It was dark inside. I thought I was probably supposed to do No Barks, but I couldn't manage it.

Lucas! I wanted Lucas! I wanted to do Go Home and get a treat and have Lucas and Mom tell me all about what a good dog I was. I wanted a T-i-i-ny Piece of Cheese.

The truck growled and started to move.

Where was I going? Why wasn't Lucas with me?

8

At first it had seemed that Hat Man was a friend—the kind of friends who carries treats. Then he'd put that strange leash on me and shut me in this crate, so I figured I'd been wrong. He wasn't any kind of friend at all.

But then the truck stopped. The back door opened. Hat Man stood there, shaking his head.

"Can't believe I'm about to do this," he muttered.

We were home! I lifted my head and started to wag. When Hat Man opened up my crate and slipped that strange leash over my head again, I let him.

He'd taken me back to Lucas, so he was a friend after all. Even if he did have the worst leash ever.

Hat Man tugged on the leash and I jumped to the ground. He took me up to our door and knocked on it.

Lucas opened it. Lucas! I jumped up on him, panting

into his face to tell him all about how I'd chased the squirrel and gone for a car ride and could he get this uncomfortable leash off my neck, please?

He did. And then he and Hat Man talked. Lucas didn't seem as happy as I was to be back together. I licked him a lot to remind him of how nice it was whenever we were near each other.

"You need to understand," Hat Man told Lucas. His voice was stern. "I broke the rules to get her back to you this time. I can't do it again. If any animal control officer sees her outside, we have to pick her up and she'll be put down." He pulled his hat down more firmly on his head. "You need to get her out of town *now*."

Mom came home, and Mom and Lucas talked. Then Mom and Lucas talked into their phones, almost as if they'd forgotten that they had a dog right here to play with. It was very strange. Nobody seemed happy at all. When I licked at Lucas's face, it tasted salty and damp.

"Mom, she's going to think I abandoned her," he said. Then he sat down on the floor and hugged me very tightly.

I wiggled out of Lucas's grip and went and got my ball and dropped it in his lap. A ball would definitely make him happier.

But it didn't.

After a little while, the doorbell rang. It was very hard to do No Barks, but I did it. I sat right at Lucas's feet to be sure he noticed and would give me the treat that I'd earned.

"Oh, Bella," he said. He gave me a whole *handful* of treats!

Audrey and Olivia came in the door, and I charged to greet them and wag at them. How nice. More people to pet me and be happy with me!

"We came as soon as we could," Audrey said. "I'm so sorry. What a terrible situation."

"I hate that stupid law!" Olivia said angrily. She sat down on the floor with Lucas and me and picked up one of Lucas's old socks for me to tug on.

"We all do," Audrey said. "But we can't change it right now. The important thing to do is to keep Bella safe."

"You can help us?" Mom asked. "We just need a few more weeks to find a new place to live."

Audrey nodded. "My sister Loretta lives about seven hours away. They don't have a pit bull ban in her city. She and her husband can take Bella for a little while."

I pulled the sock right out of Olivia's hand. Yes! I won! I took the sock to Lucas and laid it down on his lap. More playtime, please?

But Lucas didn't pick up the sock. He looked at Mom, and his face crumbled. He was in such misery that I wanted to bark to chase away whatever was hurting him.

He put his arms around me again. He pressed his face against my shoulders. I squirmed around so that I could lick him. I mostly found an ear and a bit of cheek.

I did not understand all the sadness. We were home!

We were together! I'd been a good dog! Couldn't we do T-i-i-ny Piece of Cheese?

"We'd better take her now," Audrey said. Her voice was gentle.

Lucas hesitated. Then he let go of me and took his face out of my fur. He went to find my leash and I shook myself happily. We were going on a walk! Nobody could be sad on a walk!

Lucas walked me outside to the street. Audrey and Olivia and Mom came, too, Mom leaning on her special stick. Oliva carried a blanket over her arm—my Lucas blanket.

But we did not go on a walk after all. Audrey opened up the back of a car, and there was a crate inside it. Olivia put my Lucas blanket inside the crate. This was very strange.

Lucas patted the blanket. "Okay, Bella. Inside," he told me. His voice was hoarse.

I looked around uneasily. I didn't really want a car ride right then. But I did what he said. I hopped up into the crate, turned around once, and lay down.

Lucas shut the door. I looked at him appealingly. I whined. I didn't like having the door of the crate between us.

"I know you don't understand," Lucas said. He was getting sadder and sadder. I whined louder. I couldn't comfort my boy inside this crate! "But I'm not abandoning you, Bella. I'll come and get you. It won't be long before you can go home."

Go Home? My whole body sprang to alertness. We were doing Go Home?

But how could I? I was stuck inside this crate and the door was closed.

Before I could figure it out, Lucas took something out of his pocket. It was a plastic bag that rustled in a very interesting way.

I sat up. Lucas pulled something out of the bag.

It was a T-i-i-ny Piece of Cheese!

I did not understand what was going on, but I was so happy and grateful to be a good dog. Whenever we did T-i-i-ny Piece of Cheese, I was good. I watched Lucas's hand carefully. He moved it up and down and in a circle. My head moved with it.

Then he reached through the bars of the cage and let me take the treat. It tasted wonderful. I licked Lucas's hand very carefully, to get every last bit of cheese there was.

Then Lucas took his hand away and stepped back from the cage.

Audrey closed the back door of the car. A minute later, the car started to move.

Lucas was not in the car!

I knew I should do No Barks, but I couldn't help myself.

9

The smells around me changed as the car kept moving farther and farther away from Lucas. Before this, I had always been aware of a combination of cars and people and animals and smoke and dirt and growing things, but it was only a background for the smells that really mattered: Mom and Lucas and me and the home where we all lived together.

But now, as we drove, that background smell seemed to gather itself together on the wind, like a scattering of dogs coming together to form a pack. I could no longer smell Lucas or Mom or our apartment, but I could still smell everything that surrounded them. That smell was important. It was the smell of Go Home.

When Audrey stopped and let me out of the crate so that I could pee, I lifted my head once I had finished.

The wind rushed passed my nose, and I could pick out that familiar smell among all the others.

That way, I thought, pointing my nose. *That way lies Go Home.*

That way lies Lucas.

But we were not going that way!

Now that I knew to locate the gathering of odors on the wind, I could track other, different gatherings. Audrey and Olivia kept saying the word *town,* and that's eventually how I thought of the combination of people smells and animal smells and smoke and cars—towns, each one similar to, but different from, where I lived with Lucas.

There were so many!

Audrey and Olivia took me to a house. Inside the house was a man named Uncle José and a woman named Aunt Loretta and a big dog and a little dog and two cats and a big white bird.

Audrey and Olivia talked to me and petted me, but it was hard to even pick up my head to look at them. Every part of my body felt heavy with sorrow.

"Oh, look, she misses Lucas so much already," Olivia said. "Poor Bella."

Audrey and Olivia spent the night. The next day, they got back in the car and drove away. I was left behind.

That first day, I was too miserable to eat. The next day was the same. Mostly I lay on my Lucas blanket, breathing in his smell and missing him so much it hurt.

Then I thought about Lucas. Thought about who he was, how much he loved me, how he would praise me when I was a good dog. I lifted my head as if he were right there, reaching his hand out.

He would come for me here. I was sure of it. If I was the very best dog I could be, Lucas would come and get me. The thought made me feel better, so I got off of my Lucas blanket and began to explore.

The little white dog was named Rascal, and he had never been taught No Barks. The big brown one was named Grump, and he was very old and slow and liked to sleep most of the day. The bird lived in a cage and had a high voice. "Sit!" it told me when I sniffed its cage.

I had never met a bird that could talk before! Bewildered, I did Sit. The bird did not give me a treat. It also did not seem to notice that I was a good dog doing exactly what it told me to do, because it kept saying "Sit!" at me. After a while I gave up and moved on.

What kind of place was this, where the birds were in charge?

The cats ignored me unless I approached them too closely, and then they snarled. What sort of place had cats who didn't want to play with me?

I did not feel that I belonged here.

Uncle José mostly sat in a big, soft chair. He liked to eat food out of a bowl and would slip me a piece of salty treat when Loretta wasn't nearby.

I spent a lot of time doing Sit by Uncle José's chair.

I knew that if he gave me treats I was being a good dog, the way I knew I was being a good dog when Lucas and I did T-i-i-ny Piece of Cheese. If I was a good dog, Lucas would come to get me.

Aunt Loretta smelled of soap and food and was very nice. She told me I was a good dog and let me out into a big yard in the back of their house, with a high fence all around it made of wood. I could go into this yard without my leash on, which was different from when I lived with Lucas and Mom.

Near the fence there was a structure like the ones I used to see at the park—a slide plus a swing that dangled down from a bar overhead. The slide made me think of Lucas, so I went over to it and sniffed it. But it did not smell of him.

I looked at Aunt Loretta, in case she had a ball to throw up the slide for me. But she did not know how to play.

"That's a swing set. Do you smell something interesting on it, Bella? Our grandkids sometimes use it," Loretta told me. "But they're in school now. Want a treat, Bella?"

Treats were nice. But I wanted Lucas more.

Trips to the backyard gave me a chance to explore with my nose what I had learned during my car trip with Audrey. Out in the world, beyond the fence, there were many homes and dogs and cars. Some were bunched together into towns. I could tell the difference between them—they each had their own unique set of odors.

Only one town was the right one. Only one town smelled like Go Home. In the backyard, when I lifted my nose, I thought I could find the scent of it. It was far away and faint, but it was there.

That was where I needed to go. That was where Lucas was.

Sometimes Aunt Loretta and Uncle José would put me on a leash and take me for walks along a path near the backyard. "I love living right up against the state forest, Bella. Isn't it fantastic?" Loretta asked me once. I could sense that she was very happy, but she didn't let me off the leash. So whatever was going on, it couldn't be *that* wonderful.

I wagged a bit to show her that I was listening, but my nose was very busy. On the wind, from both near and far, I could smell plants and trees and water and many, many animals. Not just dogs and cats—animals I had never met.

"Audrey called," José said from behind us.

"Oh?"

"They said Bella's owner found a new apartment in a pit-friendly town. So they can come and get her."

I wagged a little for my name, but they didn't seem to be talking to me. Nobody petted me.

"Oh, that's such good news."

Uncle José caught up to us and bent down to rub my ears. "Hear that, Bella? Your people are coming to-morrow. I'll miss you. You've been good company. But I bet you'll be glad to go home."

My ears perked up. My tail grew still.

Uncle José had just told me to Go Home.

But Aunt Loretta still had hold of my leash!

I pulled against the leash. I whined. I wanted nothing more than to run and run and run until I was Go Home with Lucas. But even though Uncle José had told me to do Go Home, Aunt Loretta did not let me go.

"Bella, come on!" she said, tugging on the leash.

Once we got back, I lay on my Lucas blanket in the living room. Rascal came and flopped down next to me. I closed my eyes. I thought of Lucas.

I thought of all the games we played—like T-i-i-ny Piece of Cheese and Ball and Go Home.

Go Home.

I was trying to be a good dog, but Lucas had not come to get me.

I remembered when Lucas placed my Lucas blanket in the crate in Audrey's car. He said Go Home. Maybe I wasn't a good dog because I was still here, because I hadn't done what he said. And today, Uncle José said Go Home.

So that's what I would do.

L ater that day, Uncle José went out in the backyard to push a strange-smelling, noisy metal machine back and forth across the grass. I went with him to watch, even though I didn't like the sound the ma-

chine made. He sure loved taking that thing for a walk in the yard!

He tugged the slide across the yard so that he could push his loud machine over the ground where it had been. Then the machine went silent and he dragged it into the garage.

A rough wind brushed at my face and ruffled my fur and made the swing move gently back and forth. I could smell so many things out there, but I could not smell Lucas.

Still, I knew where he was. I could sense him. It was like a pull on a leash, a leash I could not see but could feel all the same.

Uncle José came out of the garage and went to the house. He opened the door.

I could not climb the fence. It was too high to jump over.

I wanted Lucas. If Lucas was here, he would throw a ball for me and it would bounce up the slide and I would chase it.

Since Uncle José had moved the slide, it was up against the fence. If Lucas threw a ball right now, it would go up the ramp and over the wooden fence. I would chase it and then I'd jump. When I caught the ball I would be on the other side of the fence.

"You coming, Bella?" Uncle José called to me.

Then I realized that I did not need a ball. I could run up the slide all by myself!

"Bella?"

I didn't wait for a moment. I raced across the yard and up the slide and sailed over the top of the fence!

On the other side, I landed lightly on some soft dirt. "Bella! No!" Uncle José yelled.

I left the house and the yard and Aunt Loretta and Uncle José and Rascal and Grump and the cats and the talking bird behind me. *Lucas!* I went toward the path that led to the trees and the dirt and the smell of water and animals and space. I felt strong and good and alive with a purpose.

I was a good dog. I was doing Go Home.

I walked along the path until the light went away and darkness came. Then I curled up under a bush, but I could not sleep. I had never been alone outside before. The night was full of sounds and odors and loneliness.

I wanted my Lucas blanket. Lying in a pile of leaves was not the same.

When light came, I continued to follow the trail. It led to another that smelled as if many people and some dogs had walked on it. Whenever I heard anyone coming near, I turned and trotted away from the path and lay down until they had passed.

Somehow I knew that I should not let people who were not Lucas find me.

There was a stream near the path, and I drank from it several times. But after a little while I began to feel hungry. It was a new kind of hunger, one I had not felt before.

My stomach was empty and it ached a little. I wanted Lucas or Uncle José or Aunt Loretta to fill up my bowl with food. I wanted Lucas to do T-i-i-ny Piece of Cheese with me. I licked my lips, thinking about it.

When the day began cooling and turning dark, I was exhausted. I knew I needed to sleep even though I had not found Lucas yet, so I dug a hollow by a rock and curled up.

I was cold and sad and alone. Doing Go Home had never taken this long before.

10

A shocking scream jolted me awake. I jumped to my feet. It was still dark, and whatever had made the noise was close by.

The scream came again, and I twitched and turned in a circle. There was no pain or no fear in the cry—I could tell that—but I did not know what kind of animal might make a noise like that.

Another sound came, hard and loud, like a dog letting out a single bark. But this was no dog. I needed to learn what was making this sound, so I shook myself and padded off into the dark to find out.

I slowed as my ears told me I was close. But the breeze was flowing away from me and I couldn't smell what I was approaching.

Then I saw it in the moonlight—something that

looked like a large dog sitting on a boulder. Its mouth yawned open and a shrieking call filled the night.

But this animal was not a dog, not quite. It did not smell exactly like a dog, and its ears were odd and pointed, and its tail was heavy and bushy.

The not-quite-a-dog whirled and stared at me.

I felt the fur rise on the back of my neck. This animal reminded me of squirrels. Squirrels did not live in homes or wear collars or go on walks. They were wild.

This animal was wild, too. What did it think of me—a good dog who lived with people? It must be jealous of me, I decided.

The strange creature leaped silently to the ground and dashed off into the trees. I watched it go.

What other creatures were waiting out there in the dark forest?

I went back to my rock and slept some more. In the morning, when I woke, I was worried, hungry, and a little afraid. I knew I was being a good dog to do Go Home, but the path I had been following did not lead directly there.

If I stayed on the path, I would not go straight to Lucas. If I left it, I would have to walk over rocks or push my way through plants and bushes. It just seemed easier to stay on the trail. But I felt anxious about it. I hoped Lucas would not think I was a bad dog.

After a time, the trail began to slant downhill, and the smell of people drifted to my nose. These people were not Lucas or Mom, but I wanted to be nearer to them. I was lonely out here, with no people of any kind.

Now I heard the voices of two boys. I turned in their direction.

When I came over the top of a small rise, I saw the boys standing by a wide, shallow stream. One of them bent and skimmed a rock over the water. It hit the surface and bounced several times.

"That's five!" the second boy called out. He was wearing a sort of sack on his back. Lucas sometimes wore a sack like that when he said *school* and left the house, and I had to do No Barks.

Sack Boy threw a stone, too, and then he straightened up and saw me.

"Hey! A dog!" He slapped his legs. Sometimes people did that when they want a dog to move closer to them. I was happy to oblige.

I sniffed at the hand Sack Boy held out to me. He was not Lucas—he was older, and taller, and his voice was deeper. But he was friendly. Soon both boys were patting me and talking to me.

"How are you, girl, huh?" Sack Boy asked. "What are you doing way out here? Are you lost?" I sniffed his hands carefully. He did not have any food in his pockets, but his fingers smelled as if they had been holding some kind of meat recently. I licked them to make sure. Yes! This boy had been holding dog treats not long ago!

"So what now?" asked the other boy.

"I've still got some beef jerky back at the car."

"So?"

"So I bet I can get her to come with us. Hey, girl, come on! Come this way!"

I went for a walk with the boys. I didn't have my leash on, so I ran ahead while they strode along the trail. I understood that now I was with these boys, just as I'd been with Uncle José and Aunt Loretta for a little while. Maybe that's how it would be from now on. I'd be with other people for a few days at a time, until I was back with Lucas at last.

I could hear the boys talking to each other, and I learned that the Sack Boy was Warren and his friend was Dude. We strolled through warm green grass to a car, and when Warren opened the car door a delicious smell wafted out.

The dog treats were in the car! We'd found the treats! I was so excited that I started spinning in circles.

"Want some beef jerky, girl?" Warren asked. I could tell he was talking to me, so I sat down to show that I could be a good dog. Warren handed me a chewy, smoky piece of meat. I gulped it down.

"She's really hungry," Dude said, watching me.

"Me, too," Warren answered him.

Both of the boys ate some of the dog treats. That was odd. With all the wonderful food that humans can pick from, why would they take treats away from a deserving dog?

"So, what, you have a dog now?" Dude asked, chewing.

Warren gave me more treats. "Dude, no way. My mom wouldn't let me have a dog."

"So what are you going to do with her?"

"Well, we can't just leave her out here," Warren said. "She probably belongs to someone. I mean, she's got a collar. We could call somebody."

"My phone doesn't work out here."

"Yeah, mine doesn't, either. Look, I know. We'll get her in the car and drive to the sheriff's office. They can call her owners or whatever."

"Yeah, sure."

All my attention was on the crinkly package in Warren's hand. There was still a little piece of dog treat in there. I wondered if he knew it. I was doing Sit, and now I shuffled my weight from one front paw to the other, to signal that such excellent behavior deserved that last tiny treat.

Warren opened the door of the car.

"Come on, girl!" he called to me.

I hesitated.

I usually liked car rides. But this felt strange. Where would Warren and Dude take me? When Audrey had put me into her car, we'd gone far away from Lucas. Would that happen again?

But then Warren rustled the bag and tossed the last dog treat into the back seat of the car, and I knew what to do. I bounded in after it. Warren and Dude got into the front seat, and that was it: we were off on a car ride.

I lifted my nose to the crack in the window, pulling in the clear, clean smells from outside. I could tell we

were heading toward a town because there were more and more scents in the air, packed closer together.

But it wasn't the right town. It wasn't Go Home.

After a while we slowed, making a few turns, and then the car stopped. I went from one window to the other in the back seat, wagging, wondering what would happen next.

"So do we just go in with her?" Dude asked.

"I dunno. No, let's leave her in the car and go in and tell them we found a dog. See what they say."

Suddenly the window next to me slid down. I could get my entire head out now!

"Why'd you do that?" Dude asked.

"Because it's sunny. You never leave a dog in a closed-up car in the sun. It heats up to, like, a thousand degrees." Warren leaned over the back of his seat and rubbed my head. "Okay, girl. You stay here, okay? You'll be okay."

I did not understand most of the words, but the tone was familiar. And so was that word *okay*. People said that word a lot when they were about to leave their dogs. "Okay, Bella," Lucas would say, "I have to go to school now."

And that's what Warren and Dude did. They got out of the car and shut the doors behind them. "We'll be back, I promise," Warren told me.

They walked into a nearby building. They were gone.

11

As I sat in the car that belonged to Warren and Dude, I began to understand something. Many people were very nice and they might even take me on a car ride or give me treats, but they would not take me to Lucas. In fact, some of them might take me *away* from Lucas.

That was not right. I needed to do Go Home.

I stuck my head out of the window and then my front paws. I wiggled my rear end, pushing myself forward, until my front paws were nearly touching the sidewalk.

My chest and my stomach scraped against the window and it hurt, but I did not stop. I pushed and pushed, and then my back paws were scrabbling in the air and I was falling nose first toward the ground.

I landed on the sidewalk in a heap. Quickly, I jumped up and shook myself.

I was out of the car and off the leash. I lifted my nose and trotted away. I would do Go Home, like a good dog, but first there was something else to investigate.

I went toward the smell of food.

There were cars and people and buildings and streets all around, so I knew I was in a town. But it was not the one where I lived with Lucas and Mom. It was not the one I had visited with Uncle José, either.

As I followed my nose, some people called to me from windows or open doorways. They seemed friendly, but I did not believe they would take me to Lucas, so I did not go close to them.

I did, however, detect something sweet on the sidewalk and I ate it quickly. Then I crunched up some dry bread next to it. What a nice town, to leave treats out for good dogs to find.

I could smell that many dogs had walked over this sidewalk, and I could hear barking in the distance. As I walked along, I saw a dog with a chain that went from his collar to the wall of a house. He barked and lunged at me. I passed him, and then I smelled something interesting—several dogs, all moving together. I headed for them.

When I rounded a corner, I came upon a pack.

In the pack there were two male dogs, one small with crazy hair that stuck out in every direction, and one big with a single tooth that poked out of his mouth even when it was closed. There was also a female with scruffy fur, a fluffy butt, and a keen, alert look in her eyes.

They were sitting behind a store, and out of that store a delicious smell poured. Saliva pooled in my mouth as I trotted closer.

All the members of the pack were staring hard at a doorway, but when I got near, their heads whipped around. Small Male ran straight at me, then pulled up, lifting his snout as he stopped. I turned so that we could sniff each other, nose to tail.

I moved stiffly, not prepared to bow and invite a play session with these strange dogs. But I wagged my tail, to show that I was friendly if they were.

Big Male moved a little bit away and lifted his leg on a railing. Small Male did the same. I politely sniffed. Fluffy Butt had not moved from where she sat. Her eyes stayed fixed on the store's doorway.

Then the back door opened, and a cloud of smells poured out—cooking meat and fresh bread and melting butter. It was fabulous. A woman stood in the doorway. "Hello, pretty dogs!" she sang out.

The males ran over to do Sit at the woman's feet. I followed, though I held back a little, careful not to crowd the other dogs.

What was about to happen? And did it have anything to do with that wonderful smell?

The woman had a marvelously greasy paper rolled up in her hands. The paper rustled—what a lovely noise!—as she reached inside it and plucked out fatty pieces of cooked beef. Starting with Fluffy Butt, she went down the row of dogs, handing each of us a large chunk.

"Are you a new friend?" she asked when she came to me. "What's your name?" She held out a delectable slice. I took it delicately from her fingers and ate it in two or three bites, so none of the other dogs would have a chance to take it from me. Nothing had ever tasted so good—except, of course, a T-i-i-ny Piece of Cheese.

"That's all I have tonight, lovies. Be good dogs!" the woman said.

She went inside and shut the door behind her.

We all sniffed the ground to see if any of us had dribbled any delicious bits of meat. Fluffy Butt approached and sniffed me all over. Small Male bowed, with his front legs flat on the ground and his rear end up, tail wagging. We wrestled for a moment, and then they all moved on.

I followed. It felt good to be with other dogs. We had greeted each other, smelled each other, played with each other. I was in the pack now.

We walked down a narrow street behind a row of buildings. There were several large metal containers that clearly contained scraps of edible things, but the pack didn't stop until we reached a square plastic bin.

Big Male reached up with his nose and knocked the lid off of the bin. Odors poured out—cheese, meat, grease, sweets. I breathed in hungrily.

Then Fluffy Butt did something amazing! She leaped up so that her front paws and head were inside the bin. Her back paws scrabbled at the plastic side. She fell

back almost at once, but now she had something in her mouth—a cardboard box. Small bundles wrapped in plastic spilled from it all over the ground.

Those bundles smelled like food!

Each dog snatched a meal and darted away from the pack to finish it off. When I tore off the plastic, there was meat and bread inside mine, coated in a tangy sauce that made me sneeze.

Fluffy Butt dove into the bin again and again. Sometimes the things she pulled out were not interesting at all—little pieces of vegetables or scraps of crumpled paper. But a few times she found more to eat. I was the youngest, so I held back, letting the two males and Fluffy Butt snatch up what they wanted. That was the rule of the pack.

Once we'd gotten all we could out of the bin, the two males trotted away. Fluffy Butt and I followed. We made our way to another door with fantastic smells behind it. I was not as hungry as I'd been earlier, when I'd met Warren and Dude in the woods. But I would still be happy to have more to eat, if anyone wanted to offer it to me.

Small Male and I wrestled while Big Male lifted his leg and left his mark on a wall. Then there was a noise from inside the door, and we all ran expectantly to it and did Sit, being very good dogs.

The door opened. "Well, hello there. Are you here for a handout?" a man called. He did not hand us treats, as the woman had done earlier. He tossed

them at us, one dog at a time. The piece of crispy, salty meat that he pitched at me bounced off my nose, but I jumped on it and gobbled it up before any of the others could get it. Bacon!

The man shut the door. "That's all I have for tonight. Go on home, now. Go home."

I stared in amazement. How did this man know about Go Home?

The pack trotted away, and I followed, but I wasn't so sure that I wanted to stay with them. I was very far from Lucas, and I had just been commanded to do Go Home.

It felt like a physical pull inside me, as if the invisible leash pulling me toward Lucas had just tightened up.

Fluffy Butt left us. One moment she was with the pack, and the next she simply turned away and trotted up a walkway toward a front porch.

And then Big Male went away too. Small Male marked a tree while Big Male went straight to a building and climbed up a few steps to a metal door. I heard a rasping sound as he dragged his claws over the door's surface. After a moment, a small boy opened the door and Big Male went inside.

The door shut.

Small Male sniffed me. He turned toward a house, and then turned back to look at me, wagging. He spun in a circle, his eyes bright.

Inside the house I could see two children. They ran past a lighted window again and again. They were playing Chase-Me.

I knew that Small Male wanted me to follow him. But I understood something now. The pack was doing what Bacon Man had said. They were doing Go Home. They had houses and families and people, just like I did.

The difference was that they were close to their homes, and I was still far away from mine.

I could not go with Small Male because my person was not in his house or his family. My person was Lucas.

I turned my nose in the direction I knew would lead me to Lucas. That way there was no town. There were hills and streams and trees, and I could smell the sharp tang of something very cold. If I wanted to do Go Home, I would have to travel through those things. I would have to be without a pack, without people, maybe for a long time.

Small Male barked once and headed toward his house. Part of me wanted to join him. He had the smell of more than one human hand on his fur, and it would be so nice to sleep on a soft bed and be petted by Small Male's people.

But I could not be with my boy and also with Small Male. I turned away from him, breathed in a deep whiff of the night, and went to find my Lucas.

12

I felt uneasy as the lights and noises and smells of the town faded away behind me. I missed the pack. I missed people.

I missed treats. Very much.

I spent the night by a river, in a place where a scooped-out spot on the ground was shaped like a dog bed. Several times I awoke at the sound or smell of small animals, but none of them came near me, and none were familiar to my nose.

The path I was on did not always take me in the direction I needed to go. But I found that, if I stayed on it long enough, it would twist back until it was headed toward Go Home.

There were people on this path, too. They always let me know that they were coming with their voices

and loud footsteps, so I knew when to duck aside into tall grass or leafy bushes.

People who were not Lucas were nice and they had food, but they would not help me to do Go Home. I knew that now.

Go Home was my job. It was up to me.

The second night after my time with the pack, I found a flat area that smelled strongly of people. Many of them had walked here and sat at the wooden tables that were on the ground.

Those people had food.

The thing that smelled most strongly of food was a tall metal barrel. I came close to it, wagging my tail at the beckoning odors.

I tried to do what Fluffy Butt had done to the plastic bin, leaping up and sticking my head inside the barrel. But all that happened was that my weight pulled the whole thing over.

I felt guilty, but not for long, because food spilled out. Delicious food.

I found chicken pieces and a thick chunk of sugary treat, and some dry biscuits that were not very interesting. The chicken crunched as I chewed through the bones, and I licked succulent juice from the inside of a plastic container.

It felt so good not to be hungry anymore. Content, I curled up under a table and put my tail over my nose. Having a full stomach made me feel safe.

The next day the trail took me steeply uphill. Be-

fore long, I was hungry again. Why was my stomach so demanding? It wanted to be fed day after day, when I just wanted to do Go Home.

I heard a strange noise—a sudden, loud, cracking *bang!* It sounded a little like a door slamming, but mostly it sounded like a noise I had never heard before.

A whiff of bitter smoke reached my nose, and a voice came to my ears. "She's got to weigh a hundred fifty pounds!" someone shouted.

I did not like the noise, or the smoke. But I was interested to see the people, or at least my stomach was interested.

I would not get too close or go for a car ride. But they might have food. It was one of the best things about humans.

I left the trail and pushed through some high grass. The sound of the voices became closer and closer. "Told you we'd get something today!" one said.

I came up a small rise. Once I crested it, I saw the men.

I was on top of a small hill, and down the slope below me was a stream. On the other side of the stream, the land rose into a much steeper hill, and the two men were hurrying down it, nearly falling over their own feet in their rush to get to the stream. Both carried long black pipes in their hands.

"At least five hundred dollars!" one of them shouted.

I started to go down the hill toward them, but just

then the wind shifted. It brought me the strong smell of an animal. And also something else.

Blood.

I turned toward the blood scent, the men forgotten. I knew deep inside me that blood meant food.

I did not have far to go. Just a few steps away, among some boulders, a creature was lying motionless.

I cautiously approached. It did not stir.

I sniffed at the blood on its chest. This animal smelled similar to a cat, but she wasn't like any cat I had ever seen. She was enormous, larger than I was. And she was not moving.

I had seen squirrels like this sometimes, on the road or under bushes. That kind of squirrel was not able to play Chase-Me. It was not alive anymore.

Behind me, I could hear the men, both breathing loudly. "I need a break!" one said.

"We better grab the thing and get out of here," the other man said. "You know what happens if we get caught poaching a cougar?"

"Well, maybe you should have thought of that before you shot it!"

Their voices were excited and anxious. I decided that I did not want to meet these men after all. I was sure they would not give me any treats if I did.

A movement in the nearby bushes caught my eye. There was something there, an animal, but the wind was blowing the wrong way for me to smell it.

I stared, seeing round eyes and pointed ears.

Then I realized what I was looking at: a cat. A big cat, bigger than many dogs I had met—although still much smaller than the dead cat lying so still.

The way she held herself reminded me of the cats in the den where I had been born. She looked like they used to when they sensed a threat—the same rigid body, the same wide-eyed stare, the lips drawn back a little from the teeth.

This cat was terrified.

There was a loud shout from one of the men, and the cat cringed and backed into the bushes and darted away. I watched the skittering way she ran, and I realized something: Even though she was as large as a small-sized dog, she was not a cat. She was a kitten. A very *big* kitten.

She did not go far before she stopped and crouched in the grass, now staring past me at the big cat with the blood on its chest.

Kittens had mothers. Where was hers? Was the huge cat her mother?

The sounds and smells behind me told me that the men were coming closer. I needed to go.

I turned and padded quietly into the brush.

The big kitten followed.

As I made my way through bushes and grass, I could track the scents of the big kitten and the huge mother cat on the ground beneath me. They had come this way before me.

I did not feel happy.

I was worried by what I'd seen. I did not quite understand what had happened to the mother cat, why she lay so still, why she was no longer alive.

I did not know what the shouting men with the long black pipes had to do with all of this, but I felt that they were somehow connected.

I was beginning to understand that not all humans are like Lucas or Mom or Olivia. Some humans are not to be trusted. I had a feeling that the men with smoky pipes were humans like that.

The big kitten padded silently behind me. I turned and looked at her. She sat down, regarding me with her light-colored eyes.

I wanted to keep going. I needed to move toward Lucas, toward my human who was safe.

I took a few steps and then looked back over my shoulder. The big kitten was still sitting there. Still looking at me.

Big Kitten was an afraid kitten. She needed my help. When I was small and young and in danger, Mother Cat had protected me. Now I felt a powerful pull to protect this kitten.

When she moved off, I followed her, even though she was going in the wrong direction. Big Kitten jumped lightly over rocks and fallen logs, and I pushed along behind her. Before long, we came to a place under some trees where the smell of the huge mother cat was strong. She had spent a lot of time here.

Another scent drifted up to my nose from the dirt

under my paws: blood and meat. Something was buried there.

I scratched eagerly at the earth. Big Kitten watched, and then came to help. Before long, we unearthed the carcass of a deer. The scent of the huge mother cat and Big Kitten was still on it.

I had no idea how this deer had come to be under the dirt, but I was hungry, and I bit into it eagerly. After a time, making no noise at all, Big Kitten also began to feed.

That night I lay down on some grass near our meal. Big Kitten came right up to me and sniffed my face. I licked her, and she tensed and backed away. But when I put my head down on the ground, she came closer once more.

Sniffing, she explored me up and down. I held still, allowing her to learn all about me.

Big Kitten began to purr, and I knew what she was going to do. Sure enough, she rubbed the top of her head against me, just as my kitten friends had done back in our den. Then she curled up against my side, and I felt the fear slowly leave her body.

Once Lucas had taken care of cats. He had fed them and brought them water.

I would look after this big kitten. I believed that it was something Lucas would have wanted me to do.

13

Big Kitten and I spent several days with the body of the deer, eating as much as we wanted. When we weren't eating, we were playing. Big Kitten liked to pounce on me, and I liked to knock her on her back and chew very gently on her head until she twisted and dashed away.

She also liked to sleep most of the day, but she would become oddly alert as the sun was going down. I'd curl up for the night and she would pad silently off into the trees. One time, to my amazement, she came back with the limp body of a small rodent in her mouth.

I wondered who gave her such a thing.

We ate it together.

When all that was left of the deer was mostly bones, I could feel a restless urge to keep moving. It was time to do Go Home.

Big Kitten went with me. I remembered how, before I met Lucas, my mother dog had been taken from me. How I had found a home with a new family, a cat family.

I was Big Kitten's Mother Cat.

I found a trail going in the right direction and headed along it. Big Kitten did not seem to like the packed dirt with its scent of human feet. She would slink along nearby, hidden by grass and bushes. I could not see her, nor could I hear her, but I could smell her. She was never very far away.

When we had been on the move for two days, I felt hunger gnawing away at my belly once more. Big Kitten was probably feeling the same thing.

How could I take care of her? How could I feed her, the way Lucas had once fed the cats?

I was worrying over this as I crouched by a stream, lapping at the water. Big Kitten came out from behind some rocks and joined me. She lowered her head and lapped silently. Cats don't seem to enjoy drinking very much. When a dog is thirsty and drinks, it's easy to tell that the dog is happy. Water flies everywhere, leaking from our jaws. Cats are so delicate it's hard to see why they even bother.

I swallowed one last mouthful and lifted my head, and the scent of blood touched my nose. I began to lick my lips as I followed it along the wind. Big Kitten followed me.

I pushed through some tall grass and saw an animal I had seen once before, sitting on a rock and screaming

out a strange bark. It was a fox, trotting across a little meadow with the limp body of a rabbit in its mouth. The fox turned its head, straining with the weight of its prey, and saw us.

For a moment all three of us were frozen. Then Big Kitten darted forward, so fast I was surprised. I leaped after her, and we both went after that fox.

The fox was as swift as Big Kitten! It pulled ahead, and I knew we were going to lose that delicious food if we didn't do something quick. I barked and lunged forward. The fox turned nimbly to head away from me— but that meant it was closer to Big Kitten, who sprang at it from the other side.

The fox leaped over a fallen log and escaped, but that didn't matter. It had dropped the rabbit when Big Kitten sprang.

We fed on the fox's kill together. We were a pack, Big Kitten and me.

We didn't often get food like that rabbit. Hunger stayed with us as we traveled, as if it wanted to be part of our pack as well.

I knew that hunger meant I needed to find humans. Humans had all the good food.

But I had to be wary, too. Not all humans could be trusted.

There were special spots in the woods where people gathered. I could smell them. Sometimes the people

slept in these spots, in small dens made of some sort of cloth. Sometimes they just stopped and sat there.

But always, always, they ate.

I could easily follow my nose to these human spots. Big Kitten did not like them, and she would hang back in the trees while I approached.

One day I came near a family who were all sitting at a wooden table. A fire burned in a sort of metal pot that was high off the ground, balanced on thin legs. A man put a large piece of meat on the top of this kettle, and the amazing odor of cooking meat exploded into the air.

Nothing had ever smelled so good!

The man turned his back on the meat, talking with the people at the table, and I knew it was my chance.

I bolted out of the woods, skidded to a stop, raised up on my back legs, and nipped at the piece of meat. I didn't even burn my nose! The meat fell to the ground and I snatched it up and ran back.

None of the people even looked my way, except one. A baby sitting in a little plastic chair stared at me wide-eyed and waved tiny legs in the air, but none of the others saw what I had done.

I expected to feel like a bad dog, but I didn't. I was hunting. This meat was my prey. I shared it with Big Kitten, and it drove the hunger out of our pack for a little while.

I was doing Go Home to Lucas, but along the way I was taking care of Big Kitten, the way he would have wanted.

Another day, I followed the smell of a human to find a man standing in a stream, waving a long stick at the water. On the bank beside him was a basket full of wet fish.

I trotted over, picked up the basket, and headed back toward the woods.

The man yelled at me from the water, and even though he didn't say I was a bad dog, I could hear anger in his words. He began to scramble out of the stream, coming after me.

I picked up my pace, but the basket of fish was heavy, straining my neck and my jaws. I hoped I wouldn't have to drop it as the fox had been forced to drop the rabbit.

It turned out that I didn't have to. The man slipped on the rocks beneath the surface and, still yelling, fell flat on his back in the water! Once I was far away from him, deep into the trees, Big Kitten and I shared all of the fish. It felt so good to have a full stomach.

Most of the time when I smelled people, I found that they had already left by the time I reached the human spot. That was all right, because they left their food behind, in tall metal cans.

I became very good at knocking these cans over and picking through paper and plastic to find the feasts hidden there. Big Kitten did not come with me, but if I found something big enough to carry, I would take it back to her.

Finding food took a lot of time, and so our progress toward Lucas was slow. It was made even slower when

we heard people and had to hide. I was sure that Big Kitten did not want to go for a car ride any more than I did.

I often smelled dogs, too, but I didn't think Big Kitten would want to meet them. I longed to greet them and play with them, but they were with their people, just like I would be with Lucas someday soon.

One day I smelled dogs without humans, but I did not want to find these dogs and play with them. There was something wrong with their smell. The fur on my neck rose as I sniffed it.

I could smell that they had never had a bath. I could smell that they did not eat dog food and that no human had ever touched their fur.

I could also tell that they were tracking us, and they were getting closer.

Big Kitten and I were crossing a flat stretch of ground scattered with rocks and a few small trees. I stopped and turned to look behind. Big Kitten stopped, too.

There was a small pack of the creatures, a female and three young males. I thought of them as small, bad dogs. They were wild creatures, like the fox, but these were larger and more dangerous. They slunk toward us, low to the ground, and I knew they did not want to greet us or play with us. They were hunting us.

Big Kitten's eyes turned dark. Her lips parted, show-

ing her teeth. She was nearly as large as I was now, and we were both bigger than the small dogs, but I knew deep down that a pack of this many small animals was more powerful than a pack of two large ones.

We needed to run, but we couldn't. Behind us a steep wall of rock jutted out of the earth's surface. We could not possibly climb it. A few trees grew near its base, but they did not have trunks thick enough to hide behind.

Ahead of us was the threatening pack, now spread out across the ground to block us from escaping. I let out a low growl. This would be a fight.

The small dogs came forward cautiously. It was easy to see what they wanted. They planned to kill us and eat us.

I growled again, facing the danger.

14

As the killers approached, I felt a new kind of anger rising up inside me, a fury that made me tremble all over. These small, bad dogs were my enemies. I wanted to face them down, to fight them, to drive them away.

Big Kitten did not share my rage. I could feel and smell the terror in her. Her leg muscles bunched up underneath her body. She was going to run.

But running would not work. This was a pack, and a pack would chase. The rock wall behind us was unclimbable. If Big Kitten ran, it would be along the ground. The bad dogs would cut her off, and then they'd have her cornered.

Big Kitten did not understand the threat. She crouched down low and sprang away, racing along the

base of the rock wall. The bad dogs knew exactly what to do when prey ran.

They chased her.

I barked anxiously and raced after Big Kitten as well. When they caught her, she should not be alone.

Big Kitten was fast, but the bad dogs were faster. I could not catch up in time. Now she had almost reached a stand of two or three small trees that grew close to the wall. I was running as quickly as I could, but the small dogs were almost on top of her. Their lips pulled back, their heads snaked forward, and their teeth were bared, ready to bite.

Then, somehow, Big Kitten bounded out from underneath them. It was exactly the way she bounded out from underneath me when we played—I'd almost have her, and then, with a twist and a leap, she'd be gone.

Big Kitten seemed to soar through the air toward one of the trees. Her claws snagged the trunk and she scampered nimbly up to a branch. Big Kitten could climb like a squirrel!

The bad dogs milled about, confused, looking up at their prey. Their tongues lolled. They backed away from the tree as if afraid that Big Kitten would leap down on them.

I didn't pause, heading straight for the base of Big Kitten's tree. I would make my stand there. I would protect her from this deadly threat.

The small dogs swiveled their heads toward me. I was alone. They were a pack.

I slowed a little, bracing myself. I had not reached the tree yet. This would not be easy.

The three males slunk toward me, cutting off my path toward the tree. When they were close enough that I could have reached them in two or three leaps, they backed off, dancing away.

The female stayed by the tree, glancing at me and then up at Big Kitten. Big Kitten hissed down at her, showing all her teeth.

I eased sideways so that the rock wall was at my back. The three males closed in again and then moved away. I knew that they were trying to lure me out so that they could set upon me from all sides.

My growling turned to barking, rage forcing itself into my voice. I lunged forward, but the small dog in front of me dodged away and another leaped at my side. I turned to face this attack, and a third bad dog came from the other side. The one in front danced tantalizingly close to my jaws and backed away again.

What were they doing? Why didn't they fight?

I ached to chase them, to bite them, to feel their fur in my mouth. But I didn't want to leave Big Kitten in her tree. Sooner or later, she would have to come down, and she would need me here to defend her.

Lucas would want me to save Big Kitten.

The small dogs were silent, but I went on barking fiercely, letting them know how big I was, how power-

ful, how angry. One darted in from the side, and I snapped at him. But my teeth bit only air. Then I spun and charged at another of the males who had leaped in from the other side. This time my teeth drew blood.

The small dog screamed and fell back.

I stood with my legs braced, my head low, while the threatening pack paced back and forth in front of me. Now they knew I was not easy prey. But they were not frightened enough to leave.

They still thought they could kill me.

Then I smelled something new on the air. The noses of the small dogs lifted as well. They smelled the same thing.

People.

"Hey!" a man's voice shouted.

Several men burst from the trees, sprinting toward us across the flat ground. The small dogs wheeled and ran away, the males first, the female following. I chased them for a few steps, but I did not want to leave Big Kitten alone. I barked after my retreating enemies and swung back to return to the tree.

The men were breathing hard and slowing down. They had big sacks on their backs like the one Lucas wore when he said *school* and went away. They dropped these on the ground and came closer to me.

"Is she hurt?" I heard one of them pant. He had on a brightly colored shirt and he used it to wipe his face.

"Hey! Here, dog, here, doggie!" another called. His

face was furry. I had not met a human with fur on his face before.

Above me, Big Kitten crouched down low on her branch. I heard her claws gripping the wood tightly.

I watched the men warily. Which kind of humans were these? The kind who were not safe? The kind who would take me farther away from Lucas?

Or the kind who might have food? At that thought, I swished my tail back and forth.

"Look! Look in the tree, the tree!" the man in the bright shirt called out suddenly.

"Is it a bobcat?" the man with the furry face asked.

"No, it's a cougar, a young cougar!"

I heard Big Kitten move and looked up again. Her eyes were large and her ears were flat as she watched the men. Her fear was so powerful it made the air around us feel tense.

Her muscles bunched and knotted underneath her fur, and suddenly she sprang from the tree. She landed without a sound on top of the rock wall and vanished in an instant, darting behind some boulders.

Big Kitten! I ran to the base of the rock wall and barked, but I could not climb after her. The wall was far too steep.

"That was amazing!" the man in the bright shirt shouted.

"Here, girl, are you hurt? Did the coyotes hurt you? You okay?" asked another man. He carried a stick in

each hand, reminding me of Mom. He set down one of the sticks and reached out in a friendly way.

I hesitated.

Should I chase Big Kitten? Should I go closer to these men? The man who was holding out his hand to me sounded kind. His voice was gentle. He crouched down so that he was low to the ground, on my level.

I edged toward him. When his hand was close enough, I licked it. I tasted some fish oil and dirt on his palm.

"She's friendly," he said.

He pulled a package from his pocket and fed me treats, small pieces of meat. They tasted so wonderful that saliva flooded my mouth. I was sorry Big Kitten could not have any, but that was not something I could fix right now. I did Sit to keep the treats coming.

"What are you doing way out here, girl?" the man with the furry face asked. He scratched behind my ear, and I leaned my head into his hand. It had been such a long time since I'd felt a human's hand in my fur.

"Look, she's got a collar. She's not a stray," the man with the sticks said. "She's lost."

"You want to take her with us?"

"Well, we can't leave her out here by herself."

I went over and sniffed at one of the sacks on the ground, reminding the men that there were snacks inside that could be shared with a good dog. I did Sit again, being good.

"She sure looks hungry," Furry Face said.

"You want to give her one of those tuna packs?" Stick Man said.

"Yeah, let's do that. Then I bet she'll follow us anywhere."

Shirt Man crouched down and took a shiny package out of a sack. He opened it up, and the air was full of a delicious fragrance of oily fish.

He put chunks of fish on a rock and I ate them as fast as I could. Then I looked up with my tail wagging hard. More?

"How far to the campsite?" asked Furry Face.

"Maybe two miles yet."

"We better get going, then."

15

The men picked up their sacks and put them on their backs. It did not look like there would be any more fish. Humans are wonderful and they can always find food, but sometimes they don't understand how much a dog can eat.

They did not put me on a leash or call me, but the way they looked at me suggested that they wanted me to follow them. I got in line behind them, and soon we were back on a path.

But they were walking in the wrong direction, away from where I needed to go. Away from Lucas.

I felt torn inside. I needed to do Go Home. But that fish had been so good . . .

I followed the men.

We walked and walked and then crossed a small

stream. The breeze drifting over the water brought me the scent of Big Kitten. She was nearby.

The men did not seem to notice her. People are like that. They often don't seem to realize when something marvelously smelly is right there. They'll walk past the most amazing odors without pausing.

That is why every person should have a dog with them. We don't miss such things.

Just as the light began to fade from the sky, the men and I reached a place where a truck was parked. Little cloth dens had been set up, and I could smell the men on them. This was a place they had been before.

There was a big plastic box, too, and the men opened it up and took food out of it. Food!

There were brown bottles that they clinked together and a sack of bread and a big plastic package with ham inside it. Ham! Wonderful ham! I did Sit over and over, and they laughed and fed me piece after piece.

I loved ham very much.

Something happened to me as I fed, though. As my hunger faded, my longing for Lucas grew. The need for food had pushed away my need for Lucas, and now the need for Lucas was pushing back. I decided that very soon, Big Kitten and I would be back to doing Go Home.

I just wanted a little bit more of that ham.

Furry Face reached out and took hold of my collar

with one hand while he gave me a piece of ham with the other. "Let's see," he said, and gave the collar a tug so that it slid off over my ears.

"Her name's Bella. Hey, Bella, you like ham, huh?" he said. "Want some more?"

"Is there a phone number?" the man with the sticks asked.

"Yep. We can call when we get somewhere with decent reception."

"Good. I wouldn't want to take her to a shelter. She's a good girl. Bella, you're a good girl, right?"

I wagged. I liked these men. They knew my name and understood that if I did Sit it was important to give me ham.

"That cougar was amazing, huh?" Shirt Man said. "I never saw one before."

"Looked like a cub to me. That's even more rare," said Stick Man. "I've never seen coyotes before, either."

"A cub? No way! Full grown, or almost," said Furry Face.

I nudged at his hand, which still held my collar, so he'd remember I was still being a good dog and doing Sit.

"Thing was huge! What do you mean, a cub?" asked Shirt Man.

"No way. You just thought it was huge because you were scared," said Stick Man.

"Scared? You're nuts."

"If it comes back, you know what to do, right? You

get up on something, like a picnic table or a rock or the cooler, and lift your arms up. Spread out your jacket if you can, so you look really big. That'll make them back off."

"Why?" Shirt Man asked.

"I don't know," Stick Man replied. "Maybe they think you're a bear or something."

Furry Face snorted. "I'm pretty sure they can tell you're a tax accountant."

"Okay, sure." Shirt Man looked around a little anxiously. "You think it's going to come back?"

"Cougars stay away from people, mostly."

"Mostly?"

I heard a faint crack out among the trees, as if a dry twig had snapped when something stepped on it. I sniffed. The odor of ham was the strongest thing I could smell, but I could also tell that Big Kitten was still there.

"What was that?" Shirt Man asked.

"What was what?"

"Didn't you hear a noise?" Shirt Man dug into a pocket and pulled out a flat, rectangular black box—his phone. He thumbed it and a bright light sprang out of it. He shone the light into the trees.

Yellow eyes stared back.

Big Kitten was halfway up a tree, clinging to the trunk with all four feet. She froze, her eyes wide. Her ears went flat against her head. Her mouth opened in a snarl.

"Yahhhh!" Shirt Man yelled and dropped his phone. Both he and Furry Face tried to jump on the cooler at once. They smacked into each other and fell sprawling into the dirt.

When he fell, Furry Face dropped my collar and the ham.

"Get up, get up!" Shirt Man cried frantically.

Stick Man was already running for the pickup truck. The other two men staggered to their feet and joined him. All three dove into the back of the truck.

Big Kitten leaped off her tree and disappeared into the bushes. She had been brave to come this close to the men. Now that they were running and shouting, she was terrified.

I looked at the men huddled in the pickup truck. I looked at the ham in the dirt.

It didn't seem as if we were doing Sit anymore. I picked up the ham in my teeth and trotted off in the darkness to find Big Kitten. Our pack was together again.

Over the next several days, Big Kitten and I did not manage to find any humans who could feed us. There were plenty of streams and pools, so we were not thirsty, but my stomach was in pain all the time.

We hunted, but Big Kitten was terrible at it. She didn't seem to notice the scent of any animal, even the most obvious. At least she did learn to understand

when I was tracking prey, and she would follow me closely. But even if I got close enough to flush a rabbit or a squirrel or a mouse out of hiding, she didn't chase it!

Often she would just crouch in the grass or among the rocks, nearly invisible, watching me tear after our dinner. It was irritating. She just did not understand how to be part of a pack.

I could smell towns, but they were too far to do us any good. All I could think of was metal cans full of discarded meat and soggy bread, or doors opening so that people could hand out bacon. But we could not find any of those things here.

My strength began to fade. I had to lie down and take lots of naps during the day. In the nighttime Big Kitten would often leave my side to prowl around, but I slept without stirring until light.

I was so exhausted that when I saw a rabbit hop by one morning, I almost forgot to chase it. Then I surged forward, and the tiny creature ran and turned and bounded and fled straight toward Big Kitten.

Big Kitten shot out one paw and smacked the rabbit hard. It went tumbling and she pounced.

She had it! Prey! Food!

We devoured it side by side.

The rabbit didn't make the hunger pain go away, but it did give me strength. Early the next morning I woke up with some energy. I lifted my head and sniffed.

What was that smell? That amazing smell?

It was blood! Blood and fresh meat!

Big Kitten was sleeping beside me. She lifted up her head, too, catching the same scent on the breeze. Together we rose and followed the trail on the air.

Before long we came upon a grassy area surrounded by trees. Lying in the grass was a deer with a long, smooth stick jutting out of its neck.

The smell of humans was strong on the stick, but I could not see or smell any humans nearby. And the deer was dead.

The deer was food.

I was prepared to start eating at once, but Big Kitten did something very odd. She seized the deer in her jaws and began dragging it away. Was this some sort of game? Why play a game with food when we were both so hungry?

I followed Big Kitten. She did not stop until she came to a patch of sandy soil by a boulder. She dropped the deer, and we finally fed. I ate until my stomach was so full it was almost painful. All I wanted to do now was sleep.

For some reason Big Kitten didn't join me as I stretched out in the sun. She scratched and dug at the dirt until our kill was completely covered over with sand, leaves, and grass.

What an odd thing to do to perfectly good food.

When she was finished, Big Kitten lay down beside a large boulder, nearly hidden in the grass. I fell asleep listening to her purr.

We stayed with the deer for several days, feeding,

making trips to a small stream to drink, and then coming back to rest. I knew I wasn't doing Go Home as I should, but the lure of food was too strong to resist.

At last we had finished the deer down to the bones. Bones are good, too, but not good enough to keep me away from Lucas.

It was time to do Go Home again.

I found a trail for us to follow, one where human feet had walked. Big Kitten, as usual, did not stay with me on the trail, but she followed close by.

We had strength in us from the deer, strength enough that we did not need to eat for a day or two—maybe a little more. Maybe we had enough strength to take us all the way to Lucas.

But then something happened that changed everything.

16

When I woke one morning, the sky was just starting to lighten, and the world was completely different.

A heavy white layer of Snow Do Your Business, thicker than a dog bed, lay on the ground. Wet flakes poured from the sky with a faint, muffled roar.

Most of the smells that used to fill my nose had vanished, wiped out by the Snow Do Your Business, which smelled of clean, clear water and little else. Without all those scents to distract me, I could feel the pull of Go Home more powerfully than ever.

Big Kitten was not sleeping beside me. She'd gone during the night, as she often did. I got up and shook myself. Wet drops flew from my fur.

When I stepped out into the Snow Do Your Business, my paws sank. I lifted my nose and I could smell

Big Kitten coming closer. Soon she trotted out from between two trees with something gray and furry—something like a big squirrel—in her mouth.

The Snow Do Your Business did not seem to bother Big Kitten when it came to walking. Her paws barely seemed to sink into it. She walked gracefully, picking up a front foot and then putting her back foot right into the hole that the front foot had left.

She came to me and dropped the squirrel at my feet, and we fed. Then she sniffed me and rubbed her head on me, the way cats do.

I was eating many different things, now that I was taking care of Big Kitten. T-i-i-ny Piece of Cheese seemed so far, far away now.

It felt so good to have food in my stomach and my pack with me that I shook myself all over and bounded away through the snow. With each leap, I sank in deeply. Flakes flew as I heaved myself out and jumped again. A wind was picking up, so that the flakes twinkled in the air.

It was hard work, but it was fun! I barked at Big Kitten. Wasn't she going to play with me? We'd been working so hard at Go Home for so long . . . it was time for a little bit of fun.

I galloped downhill and onto a flat stretch where the Snow Do Your Business had been swept away by the wind. My paws went skidding out from under me as if each was trying to run in a different direction. Ice!

Big Kitten picked her way down the hill after me.

She touched one paw delicately to the ice and drew it back. Then she sat down and looked at me as if she did not understand that it was playtime.

I skidded and scrabbled on the ice, getting myself turned around. Then I braced myself, gripping with my claws, and launched myself across the ice, toward Big Kitten.

She was startled. She drew herself up, making herself tall.

I tried to stop and play bow in front of her so that she'd see how much fun Snow Do Your Business could be, but I could not stop. Big Kitten tried to leap out of the way, but it was too late. I plowed into her, and we both tumbled across the ice.

At last we were playing!

Big Kitten snarled and showed me her teeth. I did a play growl back at her. She rolled away and righted herself, shooting her claws out to grip the ice, and tried to run.

She fell, flat on her belly. I pounced on her. Wrestling!

Big Kitten was so big that I could not wrestle with her for long. She rolled over again and flung me off. Then she struggled to her feet and did her best to run.

I chased her. Yes! Playtime at last! But when we got off the ice and into the deeper snow, I had to give up Chase-Me because Big Kitten was so much faster. I sank into the Snow Do Your Business with every leap, while she stayed more or less on top.

We found a spot at the roots of a tall tree and slept some more. We slept the whole day, in fact, lying curled up together, sharing each other's warmth, while more Snow Do Your Business came down.

I began to get restless. Now that I could feel the sense of Go Home so strongly, I wanted to move toward it. But I could not travel with all this white stuff pouring from the sky.

When we woke in the morning, it was time to get back to work. Go Home was hard work, even harder than before.

To make a way forward, I had to break a path with my forelegs. Yesterday, the Snow Do Your Business had been fun. Today it was trying to slow me down, to keep me apart from my boy.

I missed Lucas. I ached to be with him, to feel his hand on my fur, to be called Bella again. Big Kitten was my pack now, but a pack was not a person. When I was with Big Kitten, I had no name.

I wanted a name. I wanted a T-i-i-ny Piece of Cheese. I needed my person so powerfully it was hard to sleep.

But it felt impossible to get to him. In the next few days, I struggled to move forward, but the Snow Do Your Business kept trying to hold me back.

Where I struggled, Big Kitten walked easily. It seemed as if the snowfall had reversed all the rules of our pack. She decided where to go, and I had no choice but to follow her.

The ground we were traveling grew steeper by the

day. Downhill, I could sometimes smell people and machines, smoke and food. Uphill was only the pure, wild smell of rock and ice. Big Kitten always chose up. I always went with her.

The Snow Do Your Business that made the going so hard for me somehow seemed to make hunting easier for Big Kitten. In the nighttime she often came back with some kind of food to share with me—a mouse, a rabbit, or a squirrel.

Was she finding a human to feed her? I couldn't smell any people anywhere nearby.

One morning I smelled something familiar, but it was not a person. It was *us*. Big Kitten and I had wandered in a large circle, and we'd crossed over our own trail!

We were not getting any closer to Lucas at all.

Frustrated, I plunged away from my own footsteps and charged out into the unbroken whiteness. Then I froze at the barest suggestion of a scent on the cold air.

Dog.

A dog! It had been so long since I had seen another dog!

I turned toward the scent, even though it meant walking uphill. I played with Big Kitten every day, but right now I longed to wrestle with a dog.

As I trudged upward, I picked up a new odor. Humans. I hesitated.

To see the dog I could smell, I would have to get near a human. They were together, somewhere on the mountain above me.

Two other humans were off to the side. They did not seem to have dogs with them.

Humans often had food, like ham. But even the nice ones did not seem to understand that I was doing Go Home.

I walked forward and paused and went forward again. I wanted to find this new dog. I wanted to see the people and I also wanted to stay away from them. It was hard to know what to do.

I pushed my way between two trees and saw whiteness. No trees, no rocks. Just a long steep slope, like a white wall, reaching up toward the sky.

Way, way up there a man and a dog were trudging through heavy snowfall. Above them, the wall of white continued up, ending in a ridge with sky above it. A thick layer of Snow Do Your Business sat heavily on the top of the ridge, curling over its edge.

The man was wearing very long shoes and clutched poles in his hands. I could smell that the dog was a male. I did not know why anyone would take their dog on a walk so high up a hill, but I knew the dog was happy to be with his person. I could tell by the joyful leaps he was making through the fluffy whiteness.

"Stop! Hey!" a voice shouted.

Startled, I looked around. Across the long stretch of whiteness, I could now see the two other men I had smelled earlier. They were so far away that they seemed very small. They had their hands up by their mouths.

"Get out of there!" one shouted.

"That's not safe!" the other one added.

"Avalanche zone!"

These two men sounded scared and angry. I retreated a few steps into the trees. The man high up on the hill kept walking, but his dog looked toward the noise. Then he stared in my direction, and I knew that he had picked up my scent.

"Get out of there!" both men without dogs screamed at once.

The dog barked and lunged a few steps downhill, toward me. He wanted to play! I shoved my way out of the trees and through the thick Snow Do Your Business in his direction, excitedly wagging my tail.

"Dutch!" the man with the dog shouted. "Get back here!"

The dog glanced back at his person but kept on bounding down the hill toward me.

The man lifted one of those strange, big, flat shoes. He stamped, trying to get his dog's attention.

"Look out!" one of the other men shouted.

There was an odd, low noise. The curl of snow atop the ridge crumbled to bits and fell.

The man in the big shoes jerked his head around to stare as a rumble, loud as a truck, shook the air. The ground slid beneath him and he fell, tumbling.

The sliding ground caught the man and the dog and knocked them over. They were both floundering

as they plummeted toward me, moving faster than I'd ever seen anything move, even Big Kitten.

I needed to get away. I turned and dashed for the trees, plunging in huge leaps. The booming sound above me grew louder and louder. Then something slammed into me, tossing me into the air.

I lost all sense of up and down. I was rolling and falling. I could see nothing and my paws could not find the ground.

I had just one thought as something soft but heavy slammed into my head.

Lucas.

17

And just like that, the noise was gone. I lifted my head and shook it. Snow Do Your Business flew.

I was now well into the trees, but I couldn't remember how I'd gotten there. My back legs were pinned under a layer of white stuff so heavy, it felt as if Lucas were lying across them.

If Lucas were here, he'd know what to do.

Panting, I struggled to get free. I wanted to find Lucas. I wanted him to help me, to pick me up in his arms, to get me somewhere safe. I whimpered for him, but he was too far away to hear me.

I could not move my back legs, so I strained with my front paws to drag myself forward, trying to dig out. I pulled and was able to move one leg a little, and then the other. Now I could shove with both rear legs,

and the heavy Snow Do Your Business had to let me go. I pushed and staggered forward, free, panting with exhaustion.

Just moments before, the air had been filled by a huge sound. Now there was total silence.

I looked around, trying to make sense of what had happened.

The dog! He was still out on the white slopes, uphill from me, and he was sobbing with fear. We were not a pack, but the instinct to help him still rose up inside me.

I ran toward him. The layer of white stuff underneath me was much firmer than it had been before. I did not sink down. I ran across it as lightly as Big Kitten.

The dog was just at the tree line, digging frantically. Snow Do Your Business flew into the air behind him. He was a huge dog, larger than I was, with thick, dark fur. He didn't even glance at me when I arrived at his side, just yipped and whined in distress as he dug and dug in a frenzy.

Something very bad had happened. But what? Why was this dog attacking the snow so desperately?

I did not know, but before I could think, I was digging next to him. Something was bad, and we were digging. That was all I knew.

We had not been at it very long when I smelled someone approaching. It was the two men who had shouted. They were still shouting.

"There! Over there!" one of them exclaimed. "See? They're digging!"

I kept at it. The ice was packed under my paws and it was hard to get a good hole started. My nose picked up a scent under the snow—a man, the same man whose scent was painted on the male dog.

Now I knew why we were digging. We were digging to save the man.

I hardly looked up when the two new men glided up on long shoes, holding poles in their hands. One of them was taller and had darker skin than the other. They both kicked their strange shoes off.

"These must be his dogs!" the one with dark skin said.

The men knelt next to us. Now there were two dogs and two people digging.

"Got his shirt!" gasped the first man.

"Is he alive?" asked the second.

The first man, the taller one, whipped off his mittens. "Still got a pulse!"

The men dug armloads of Snow Do Your Business away from the buried man's face. Soon they had his shoulders free. They stood up, each holding one of his arms. They hauled on the man, straining to break him out.

"Keep pulling!"

Then the two standing men fell down, and the buried man was free. The male dog licked his face, whimpering.

The taller, darker man pulled a phone out of his pocket. "No signal up here. I'll go back down to the cabin. Gavin, you stay with him."

"Okay!"

The tall man put his big shoes back on, picked up his poles, and shoved off. He went away, moving quickly in a gliding sort of way I'd never seen before.

The male dog threw himself down, squeezing his body next to his person. His tongue was out and his body was trembling.

The man lying on his back did not open his eyes, but he moaned.

"It'll be okay. He'll be okay," the kneeling man told me. He reached out a hand toward me. "Good dogs. You got him out. Good girl."

I sniffed at the hand in its big puffy mitten. The male dog squirmed even closer to his person and licked and licked at his face.

I stayed with the moaning man, the dog, and the other man, who was nice enough. He took a sack off of his back and fed both me and the other dog a piece of bread.

"Dutch, is that your name?" Bread Man asked as he looked at the male dog's collar. "Hi, Dutch!" I could tell from the male dog's reaction that this was what people called him.

"What about you? Where's your collar, huh?" Bread

Man asked me. He scratched around my neck. I wagged. Yes, I would have more bread if that's what he was asking.

After a while I heard loud machines approaching from far below. When they were closer, I could see that there were two of them, flying up toward us. Each carried two people on its back and one dragged a flat sled behind it.

Three women and one man jumped off the machines and carefully lifted Dutch's person onto the sled. They strapped him down. The man groaned loudly when they moved him, but he did not wake up.

"Is he going to be okay?" Bread Man asked one of the women.

"Depends on how long he was stuck under the snow without oxygen," she answered. "It's a good thing you were able to dig him out so quickly."

"What about his dogs?" Bread Man asked.

"Oh," answered the woman.

"Will you send somebody to get them?"

"That's not—we aren't really equipped to take care of dogs," the woman told him.

"Huh." The man put a mitten down to stroke my head, and I rubbed up against him like Big Kitten did when she greeted me. "So what's going to happen to them?"

The woman shook her head. "I guess that's up to you."

We watched as the people climbed onto their ma-

chines. With a lurch, they drove off, dragging Dutch's man on the sled behind him.

Dutch let out a cry and plunged after the machines. "Dutch! Here, boy!" Bread Man yelled after him. He shoved on his long shoes, and glided after Dutch, who had left the hard-packed area and was now sinking down with every step, just as I did when I was hunting with Big Kitten in this stuff. The man leaned down and grabbed hold of Dutch's collar.

I watched.

Bread Man had called Dutch by his name and seized his collar and was now stroking him and speaking to him in soft tones. But the man had not called me Bella. He did not know me.

I breathed in. I could not smell Big Kitten, but I knew she was out there, probably not too far away. We would find each other.

More important, I could feel the pull of Lucas.

Bread Man was looking at me. He lifted his hand to his mouth and whistled. "Come on, girl!" he shouted. "Good dog!"

I hesitated. Now Bread Man was slapping his thighs. It meant he wanted me to go to him.

I wanted to do Go Home. But it had been so long since I'd heard a human voice. And this human was calling me, telling me that I was a good dog. He was being nice to Dutch, and he had bread.

I was still doing Go Home to Lucas, and I was still taking care of Big Kitten. But right then, at that

moment, I felt the same yearning I'd felt when I lived with Mother Cat and her kitten family, the need to be with humans. In just a moment, I would return to my journey, but right now, I needed something else.

I ran to the man.

Bread Man took his sack off his back, and I wondered if he had another piece of bread. He did! He reached out for me, holding bread in his mitten, and I gobbled it up.

While I was eating, he looped something around my neck, tightening it with gentle pulls. I swallowed and realized what it was.

A rope. I was on a leash.

No! I needed to be with Big Kitten! She needed her Mother Cat! I had made a terrible mistake, giving in to the urge to be with this man and his bread. I tried to shake off the rope, backing away.

"Steady, girl," the man said gently.

Dutch was on a leash, too, on the other end of the rope, and Bread Man was holding both of us by the middle. Dutch was trying so hard to be a good dog that he was quivering with the effort. What he wanted to do, I knew, was to run after that sled, to get to his person. It's what a lost dog needs to do. It's what I needed to do.

I didn't know what Dutch was feeling, but I was miserable. Somewhere out there, Big Kitten was waiting for me to find her. But I was on a leash.

"Okay, let's try this, but go slowly. You ready? Let's go!" Bread Man said.

I was startled when, with a tug on my rope and a whispery sound, Bread Man was suddenly sliding past us on his long shoes. Dutch and I were both jerked into motion. I tried to stay close enough to Bread Man to keep the leash loose, but Dutch bolted ahead.

Bread Man fell flat on his face.

"Hey! Dutch! Stop!" he yelled.

I went to Bread Man, wagging, and sniffed at his wet face. Clearly the leash wasn't working out. Clearly he would let us go.

But he didn't. After some struggling, Bread Man got back to his feet. He looked at us. Dutch whined. I wagged.

"This is going to be harder than I thought," Bread Man told us.

We kept going. Bread Man flopped down sprawling in Snow Do Your Business a *lot*, for no good reason that I could see. But we climbed a good way down the hill. Dutch seemed to understand that we were going the same direction as the machines that had taken his person, and he was a little calmer now.

Soon I smelled Bread Man's tall friend approaching, and then he appeared on top of a small hill. "Taylor! Over here!" Bread Man called.

The friend glided down to us, and he and Bread Man talked for a while. Dutch pulled at the leash and whined, restless. I sat and breathed heavily. We'd been walking with difficulty for a while, and I was tired and sad.

"So," Bread Man's friend said slowly. "I can't help but notice that you have two enormous dogs with you."

"Yeah. The mountain rescue people couldn't take them. So I was thinking . . ."

"Oh, no."

"Well, they need to be fed. Look at the female—you can see her ribs right through her fur. I thought we could take them home and get them something to eat, and call the hospital to find out what happened to the guy who got buried in the snow. We can't just take them to an animal shelter until we know what's going to happen to their owner, right?"

The friend groaned. He reached into his pack and pulled out a knife and sawed through the rope and now, just like that, Dutch and I each had our own leash! The tall man took Dutch's. "Right. Okay. Well, the first thing to do is get about two tons of dog down off this mountain."

18

We soon figured out that Bread Man's name was Gavin, and his tall friend with the dark skin was Taylor. Well, I figured it out. Dutch didn't really care about anything but getting back with his person.

We followed them down off the mountain, and then they took us for a long car ride. I did not want to get in the car, but I knew that a good dog went where her leash took her.

I could not find the scent of Big Kitten on the air. What would Big Kitten do on the mountain by herself, without me to take care of her?

Worse, I could tell that we were not going toward Go Home. In fact, Go Home was actually behind us, in the other direction.

Eventually we arrived at a big house with hard

floors and several rooms. In one of them there was a hole in the wall filled with pieces of burned wood. I sniffed carefully at them. Dutch ignored them.

There was a backyard, too. It had a metal fence around it, and inside it there was no Snow Do Your Business and no slide up against the fence, just grass and plants and a tree with no squirrels.

There was also food. Gavin brought in a big bag that smelled delicious and filled up bowls with it. Dutch did not want to eat his, so I ate it for him.

I was grateful for the food, but I knew something that these two humans did not seem to understand. They had two dogs in their house, and neither one of us truly wanted to be there.

At the first chance, I would leave. I would do Go Home to Lucas, and catch up with Big Kitten.

After I ate up both bowls of food, Gavin and Taylor sat on the floor with me and played a game I did not understand.

"Molly? Carly? Missy?" they asked me.

I wagged my tail. Maybe all this attention would come with a treat at the end of it.

"Daisy? Chloe? Bailey? Blanche?" Gavin asked.

"Blanche! You're kidding!" Taylor fell back on the couch and held a pillow to his face, laughing loudly.

"What?" Gavin demanded.

"Who would name a dog Blanche? Let's do this a better way." Taylor moved to a table and made clicking

noises with his fingers on a toy. "Here's a list of the most popular dog names."

"Is Dutch on it?" Gavin wanted to know.

"Uh . . . doesn't look like it. But let's try." Taylor looked down at me. I looked up at him, waiting to figure out what he wanted me to do. "Ellie?"

I stared back. Was Ellie some sort of treat?

"Max? Bailey?"

"We tried Bailey," Gavin objected. "And Max is a boy's name."

"What about *Maxine*?" Taylor challenged.

"Molly?" Gavin suggested.

"Bella?" Taylor asked me.

I cocked my head. It was the first time either one of them had said my name.

"Look at that," Gavin exclaimed. "Bella! Bella!"

I turned to him. Why was he saying my name?

"Yes! Wahoo!" Taylor jumped up from the table. "It's Bella!"

I couldn't help myself. I leaped up, too, and when Gavin ran around the table yelling my name, I ran with him, barking. Dutch watched from a pillow on the floor and turned his head away.

The next day Gavin brought me a new collar and slipped it over my head. It had a tag on it that made a jingling sound.

Taylor fingered it. "So, wait, you put *our* phone numbers on it?"

"Of course! What other number would I use?" Gavin replied.

"Uh, how about the one on Dutch's collar?" Taylor suggested.

"That one's disconnected," Gavin pointed out reasonably.

From that moment, we were Bella and Dutch, two dogs living with Gavin and Taylor, both of us anxious to get back to our real people.

I waited patiently for my chance to do Go Home, but days and days went by and it didn't come. The fence in their backyard was high and there was still no slide to help me jump over it. I was taken for many walks, usually at night, but always on the leash.

Dutch was sad. He spent a lot of time with his nose to the crack under the front door, sniffing and sighing. He did not want to play with me much.

Sometimes Gavin or Taylor would get down on the floor with Dutch and put their arms around him. "You going to be okay, big guy?" they would ask.

When they did that, I could feel the knot of pain inside Dutch loosen a little. He was comforted.

One evening came, though, when both Gavin and Taylor seemed to need comforting. They sat on the couch as Taylor talked on his phone. Then he put the phone down and lowered his head.

"So what does the guy we dug out of the avalanche say?" Gavin asked.

"His name's Kurch," Taylor answered. "And he's home from the hospital. His phone's working again."

"What kind of a name is Kurch?"

"Did I name him? I don't know. Anyway, I didn't talk to him. He's still pretty banged up, I guess. But that was his sister. She didn't even know he had dogs."

I looked up from where I was chewing on a toy near the fireplace. I could feel that it was about to give way under my teeth. Soon I'd have it in shreds, which would mean that I'd won.

"Yeah?" Gavin asked.

"Yeah. She says we can bring them by next week if we want to. She didn't sound all that thrilled about it, but I guess we have to do it."

"We do?" Gavin repeated, just a little hopefully.

"Gavin," Taylor said, a little sternly. "Of course we have to take the dogs back to this Kurch person. They're his dogs."

Gavin sighed. "Yeah. I know. It's just . . ." He looked away.

They both sat there in the same way that Dutch sat by the door so often. I got up, dropping my toy to the floor, and padded over to them. I put my head in Gavin's lap because he was sad.

I liked Gavin and Taylor, even though I'd have to leave them soon. I didn't want them to be sad, the way Dutch was sad. I sighed, and Gavin rubbed my ears. I could tell he felt a little better.

"Next week, Bella," he told me, "we're going to take you back to your owner."

After several days went by, something exciting happened. Gavin gave us a breakfast with bacon in it. Bacon!

Then he and Taylor took us for a long, long walk. After that, a car ride.

The walk and the bacon were good. But neither Gavin nor Taylor seemed happy. As the car ride stretched on and on, I started to feel uneasy. We weren't going closer to Lucas; I knew that.

Then the car turned from a big road onto a little road, and Dutch went stiff. He leaped to his feet and stood, staring out the window as if he could see a squirrel.

"That's right. We're almost there, guys," Taylor said.

Gavin sighed, the way he had been doing the whole car ride.

When we stopped, Dutch pawed at the window and made a low, excited whining noise. Clearly he thought something was happening. What it was, I had no idea.

When Gavin opened the car door, Dutch shot out and up onto the porch of a small house. Gavin and Taylor and I followed.

Dutch was squirming and whining beside the door. "It's okay, Dutch," Gavin said. He knocked and then pushed the door open a crack. "Hello? Anybody home?"

Dutch shoved the door all the way open with his

nose and charged inside. I looked up at Gavin in confusion. "You're home, Bella," he said to me.

Home? Was he trying to tell me to do Go Home? If that was the case, what were we doing here?

"*Argh!* Get down, Dutch!" someone shouted from inside.

Gavin and Taylor glanced at each other and took me in.

We found Dutch in a small bedroom, lying on top of a man in a bed, wagging and licking his face. The man had on stiff, thick white pants that were so heavy he could barely move his legs. One arm was covered in the same stiff white material. I never really understood the point of clothes, but these clothes were particularly bewildering. Why would anyone put something on that kept them from moving around?

"Dutch! Down!" Gavin commanded.

Dutch dropped reluctantly to the floor.

"You dumb dog," the man in the bed said to Dutch, "you trying to put me back in the hospital or something?"

Gavin stared at him. "He was just glad to see you," he said. "I'm Gavin. You're Kurch, right?'

"Sure," said the man in the bed.

"My roommate talked to your sister," Gavin said. "We brought your dogs back."

"Yeah. Hey, Dutch." The man put one bandaged hand on Dutch's head. Dutch leaned into the touch, his eyes half closed, and I missed Lucas at that moment more than I had in a long time. "But what do you mean, *dogs?*" the man went on. "That one's not mine."

Gavin looked at me. I looked back. Car ride? Treat?

"Not *yours?*" Taylor repeated. "What do you mean?"

"Yeah, never seen that one before," the man on the bed answered.

"But . . . Bella was with Dutch when we got to you. They were both digging for you in the snow. That's how we found you," Taylor told him.

"Huh. Well, must have been a coincidence," the man said.

"A what? A coincidence?" Gavin sputtered. "So . . . Bella isn't yours?"

"Nope. No way I can take care of a dog now, anyway. Sorry you came all this way," the man replied.

There was a long pause.

"What are you saying?" Gavin asked slowly.

"I'm saying I've got eleven fractured bones, that's what I'm saying," the man said impatiently. He took his hand off Dutch's head. "Both of my legs are in casts, can't you see? I can't even take care of myself, and my sister says she can only stay another few days. I'm saying I can't handle Dutch. Sorry."

"Sorry? You're sorry?" Gavin demanded. "Dutch is your *dog!*"

"So? I was in an *avalanche!*" the man snapped. Dutch looked up at him nervously.

"Because you were snowshoeing in an avalanche zone!" Taylor shot back. "Forget it. Forget that. You're saying you don't want these dogs. That's what you're saying?"

"How many times do I got to repeat myself, here? I got enough problems as it is."

Gavin and Taylor and the man on the bed looked at each other for a long time. Dutch whined for attention. I felt like whining, too.

Then Gavin looked at Taylor, sort of the way I used to look at Lucas when I wanted a walk or a treat.

"Fine," Taylor said, nodding sharply. "Fine. Sorry to bother you, Kurch. Dutch, come."

Dutch turned his head toward Taylor. He looked back at the man on the bed.

The man moved his head to stare at the wall.

Gavin and Taylor walked out of the room. I went with them. I didn't like this place very much.

Dutch took a long time to follow us.

He kept turning to glance back down the hall. He seemed bewildered.

We went back out to the car. Gavin and Taylor stood still, gazing at each other.

Taylor shook his head. "I guess we have two dogs now," he said. "Two enormous dogs. Just like I don't remember saying I ever wanted."

Gavin grinned. He hugged Taylor. Then he knelt down and hugged Dutch, too.

"That was horrible," he said softly. "But we're going to be your family now, Dutch. I promise."

We took another car ride. Dutch didn't put his nose out of the window, not once all the way back to Gavin and Taylor's house.

19

Gavin gave us both special attention and many treats and hugs for the next several days, and I could feel the sadness seeping out of Dutch a little at a time. I kept waiting for my chance to do Go Home, but it did not come.

Days went by. Lots of days.

Sometimes there would be Snow Do Your Business, and Dutch and I would go out and pee in the soft whiteness. Snow Do Your Business always reminded me of Big Kitten, gliding gracefully on top while I blundered along, sinking with every step. Then everything would melt and the ground would be wet.

A few times Dutch did Chase-Me around the yard, abandoning his sadness for a time and just being a dog.

Then the days became warmer. The grass grew fresh and green under our paws, so we peed on that.

One day when I could not sniff any coldness in the air, Gavin and Taylor packed a lot of things into the car. Then they put Dutch and me in the back seat as well.

Car ride! Were we going back to see Dutch's person again? That was a confusing idea, because it seemed as if Gavin and Taylor were both Dutch's people now.

They were not my people, although I liked them well enough. They were simply the sort who prevented a good dog from doing Go Home, even if they were well intentioned. And they had not seen Big Kitten, so they did not know I was a Mother Cat.

The windows in the car were open just a little. I sniffed out of one, and Dutch sniffed out of the other. It was amazing to thrust my snout out of a moving car . . . like having a thousand smells packed into my nose all at once.

Then I stood up on the back seat, my entire body quivering with excitement, because one of those smells was familiar.

The car had just driven over a small hill, and the smell came to me: Go Home.

It had been a while since I had smelled Go Home like this—not since Big Kitten and I were a pack in the forest. I felt its pull. If the window had been open I would have leaped out of the car and run to Lucas.

"What's she smelling?" Gavin asked, looking back at me from the front seat where he was sitting with Taylor.

"Who knows? Raccoon, maybe deer. Fox. Skunk. Coyote. The state forest is full of them."

"I hope not a skunk."

Gavin and Taylor both laughed. Dutch wagged. I stood with my nose pressed hard to the window, breathing in Go Home, as the car drove higher and higher into the mountains.

When the car stopped, we were at a small house surrounded by trees. There was a yard, too, fenced all around, but instead of cut grass there were plants and sticks just like the rest of the forest. Gavin and Taylor took us there while they carried things from the car to the house.

Dutch lifted his leg all along the plants in the backyard. I held up my nose to the breeze and searched for Big Kitten. I could locate many animals on the wind, but not her. The next morning, Gavin and Taylor gave us both some of their bacon at breakfast. Bacon! Then they laced on big, thick boots. "Want to go for a hike?" Gavin asked us.

They attached our leashes and led us out onto a trail. This place seemed familiar. I could smell that I had never been here before, but it was very like the wilderness I had traveled through with Big Kitten— tall trees, stretches of dry grass, rocks poking through the soil.

"Let the dogs run," Gavin suggested to Taylor.

"If we see a forest ranger, we'll get a fine for letting them go off leash."

"It's worth it."

Taylor knelt down and unsnapped my leash, stuffing it into the sack on his back. Gavin did the same with Dutch.

It had been a long time since I'd been out in the open without my leash. At first it felt so strange that I stayed close to Gavin and Taylor as they walked.

After a while, though, Dutch caught some sort of scent and loped ahead. I didn't know what he had found, but I trotted to keep up with him.

"Don't go far!" Gavin called.

Dutch and I both took off, galloping down the trail. I smelled a rabbit and wondered if Dutch had ever seen one. I remembered Big Kitten helping me catch rabbit meat.

I remembered being on a long, hilly trail like this one.

I remembered Go Home. I remembered Lucas.

Dutch and I tore around a curve in the path. Thick trees blocked us from the sight of Gavin and Taylor.

"Dutch! Bella!" I heard Taylor's voice behind us.

Dutch pulled up short immediately. I stopped, too, but not to go back to the men.

Dutch and I nosed each other, panting. I wagged my tail. I liked Dutch. I liked Gavin and Taylor, too. We had been a pack together. But they were not Lucas, and now it was time for me to move on.

"Bella! Dutch! Come on!" This time it was Gavin calling.

Dutch moved toward the sound. I didn't. He stopped and looked at me, and he seemed confused. He did not understand why I wasn't heading back along the trail. Why would I run away from a wonderful life with the two men who had found us?

Dutch could not ignore Gavin and Taylor. They were his people now. But Lucas was my person, and it was finally time that I went back to him. At last I could do Go Home.

Dutch left me and ran back along the trail the way we had come, to be with his family.

I continued on in the other direction.

For a long time, I was aware of Dutch. I could smell his scent behind me as I followed the trail.

I knew he would be happy with Gavin and Taylor, and they would be all right, too, with Dutch in their family. If it had not been for Dutch, I might not have been able to leave. But I felt good, knowing that Gavin and Taylor had a dog to take care of them.

Much sooner than I expected, I was tired and thirsty. I curled up in a protected spot by a huge log and lay down, yawning.

It wasn't easy to sleep. I had forgotten all the animal smells and noises that came with darkness. A fox's scream jolted me awake a few times. I thought about Lucas, about Gavin and Taylor and Big Kitten and Uncle José and Aunt Loretta, and I missed all of them.

I could imagine Lucas touching my fur, and my nose filled with his scent, as if he were really there.

I felt very alone.

I traveled along the path for the next few days, since it was doing me the favor of pointing directly at Go Home. I waded through mossy streams and made my way through thick strands of trees and crossed a vast stretch of yellow grass. All the trees there had a black coating on their trunks that smelled of charred wood, like the wood that Gavin and Taylor would sometimes burn in the hole in their wall. Most of these trees had no leaves at all, just bare branches pointing to the sky.

The faint, wild smell of the small bad dogs came to me here. Not the same ones that had trapped Big Kitten in the tree—a different pack. Larger. Not too far away.

I went in the opposite direction.

Hunger grew in my belly, and it could not be ignored. I smelled a large lake and went toward it, but I had to cross a busy road to get there.

I felt like a bad dog, crouched in the grass by the roadside as cars and trucks roared past. Good dogs did not run across roads. I knew that.

But good dogs needed food. If I followed this road, I could smell that it would lead me to a town.

Towns had people. People had food. That was the way I went.

It was dark when I came to streets with houses and shops. I smelled food cooking, and the odors made sa-

liva rush into my mouth, but I could not see a dog pack waiting outside a door anywhere I looked. No humans came to offer pieces of meat.

I found a few cans that had food hidden inside them, but these were too tall for me to climb into.

I wandered the streets, but I could not find what I needed. At last a large building caught my attention. Light poured out through wide windows, and people were entering and leaving though big glass doors.

Many of the humans who were leaving were pushing metal carts. Metal carts full of bags. Bags full of food!

The doors into this building were something I had not seen before. Usually people had to touch a door and turn a knob before a dog could go in or out. These doors did not seem to work like that. When people walked up, the doors slid open without anyone touching a thing!

And every time they opened up, the most amazing smell wafted out. Chicken! Someone was cooking chickens in there!

Cautiously, I snuck closer and closer to the doors. None of the cart people stopped me or called to me or tried to put a leash on me. Mostly they ignored me.

"Doggie!" one little boy called. He was riding in a cart and reached down to me. His fingers smelled marvelous and sweet, but before I could go closer to lick them, his mother pushed the cart briskly away.

Someone chuckled. A man. He was sitting on the

ground beside the doors, holding a piece of cardboard in his hands.

I had not noticed him before, because my nose had been so busy with the smell of chicken. I studied him carefully. He did not smell like he had any food. He smelled of dirt and sweat and smoke.

"Hey, dog," he said.

The hair on his face and head was long and tangled. He had plastic sacks piled up next to him on one side and an old suitcase on the other.

I sat down and watched him. Sometimes people who came out of the big building tossed things to him— small, round bits of metal. They were not anything to eat, so I did not see why he'd want them.

One man stopped and handed the sitting man something wrapped in plastic. "Want a sandwich?" he asked. "Too much mayo for me."

The man sitting on the floor nodded. He took the sandwich in his hand. "Thanks," he said in a low, hoarse voice. The other man waved and went on his way.

My body had sprung to attention. That sandwich was much more interesting than little bits of metal.

On the hand that was not holding the sandwich, the sitting man wore a glove with no fingers. He stretched that hand out to me.

"Here, puppy," he said gently. "Want some?"

20

I hesitated at the offer of food. The man was sitting calmly with his hand out to me. He was not standing up with his arms ready to grab, and he did not have a leash in his hand, so he did not seem like a person who would try to keep me from doing Go Home.

Plus, he had a sandwich.

I moved slowly toward him, wagging. I did Sit to show him I was a good dog who needed something to eat.

The man seemed to recognize a good Sit when he saw it. He gave me a piece of soft bread and salty meat. I snapped it up. We shared the rest of the sandwich, a bite for him, a bite for me.

Then he scratched my neck and tugged gently at my collar. "What's your name? Can't see the tag," he muttered.

He pulled the collar off over my head. "Bella, huh?" he asked me. I wagged for my name. Most people who knew my name also gave me treats.

"What are you doing out by yourself? Are you lost, Bella?

I heard the question in his voice and nosed at his hand. *Yes, I would like more sandwich.*

"I've been lost," the man said quietly.

I nosed at his hand again.

"Want to be my dog, Bella? I could use a dog. You're not fierce, but you look fierce. You could fool people, I bet. Nobody would mess with me if I had a dog like you."

The man did not seem to have any more sandwich. I looked toward the big, bright building again. A woman was walking briskly in, and the doors swept open for her and shut behind her.

"But that wouldn't be right," the man said softly, looking at me. "You belong to someone. You've got a home, huh? Lucky dog. Better go home."

I looked back toward the man in surprise. That was what I was trying to do!

He reached toward my head with the collar, but I backed away. His words had made me feel restless. Go Home meant that I should run. I needed to run.

Plus, I needed chicken.

I moved toward the glass doors. They opened. It was almost like the way Lucas would hold the door for me after we got back from a walk. It was as if I was *invited.*

And inside the door, right in front of me, there was a rack of metal shelves. Lights on the shelves shone down on chickens wrapped in bags. Heat wafted off the shelf, bringing that smell, the delicious, amazing, wonderful smell, right to my nose.

It was like the chickens had me on a leash and were pulling me to them.

I slunk forward, into the store. Dogs were not supposed to take things on shelves. I knew that. Food on shelves and tables and counters was for people. Food in bowls and on the ground was for dogs.

But I could already taste the chicken, could imagine chewing and swallowing. I licked my lips.

Now I was right at the shelves. Right in front of the chickens.

I stood up on my back legs, trembling. I stretched my neck and reached my muzzle forward. Carefully, I took one bag of chicken with just my front teeth.

"Hey!" someone shouted.

I looked up with the bag in my mouth. A man with a white coat on was coming around from behind the shelves. He seemed angry.

I let go of the bag of chicken and it fell to the ground.

Food on the ground is for dogs!

I dropped down to all four feet, snatched up the bag, and turned around. Time to leave this nice building now.

But behind me, the glass doors were closed.

The angry man in the white coat was getting closer.

I needed to get away from him. I darted forward. "Stop! Dog!" the man in white shouted.

He was one of those people who wanted to keep me from Lucas. I could tell. So I ran, gripping my bag tightly in my mouth. But which way could I go? Only humans can tell how to get in and out of buildings.

The floor was slippery under my feet. I galloped along rows and rows of shelves, scrabbling around corners. When I tried to slow down, I just skidded on slick tiles.

The pounding feet of the man in pursuit frightened me. Up ahead, a younger man was standing on a ladder, stacking boxes on the top shelf. I squirmed past him. He wobbled and crashed to the floor, scattering his boxes everywhere!

People stared at me as I raced past. A few tried to grab me or the chicken. But it was *my* chicken now!

All I wanted was to find a quiet place for me and my dinner, but people were yelling. Yelling at *me*! I had to get away!

"Get him! Catch the dog!" the man in white bellowed from behind me.

A boy with a broom in his hands ran at me, so I turned, sliding, and dashed down a new row of shelves. A man with a cart called, "Here, boy," and seemed friendly, but I did not stop for him.

All I could smell was the bag in my jaws, and all I could feel was my panic. Everyone inside this building thought I was a bad dog!

"Hey!" another man shouted as I came to the end of

the aisle. He waved his arms at me, and I skittered to a halt and nearly fell before I could back wildly away.

"Got you!" It was the man in the white coat, right behind me!

I bounded forward, right toward the other man who was still waving his arms. I dove around his feet. His hand brushed the fur on my neck, but there was no collar for him to grab.

Behind me, the man in the white coat thumped into a cardboard shelf. Little plastic containers fell out, bouncing across the floor. He slid, crashing to the tiles in a heap.

I smelled the outdoors and raced off in a new direction.

But when I reached the place where that smell came from, I was not outside after all! I found myself in a part of the building that carried the smell of outside—dirt and plants and flowers—but was still inside. I spun in a circle, confused, still gripping my bag of chicken tightly.

Nobody seemed to be angry here, although there were people staring at me. So I dropped the bag to the floor, ripped it open, and bolted down several bites of chicken. It tasted just as amazing as I'd hoped.

Then I heard running footsteps. The angry men, including the one in a white coat and the boy with the broom, had caught up with me. I grabbed the bag and darted to one side.

The boy thumped into a table. A whole pile of

oranges rained down on the floor with soft, dull thuds. They rolled like balls, but I did not pause to chase them. I took off in a new direction, toward where I could smell fish and meat and cold air pouring from the walls.

"Get the dog!" the men yelled from behind me.

I raced past cold air full of meat smells, then past delicious bread and cheese. This place was like a giant kitchen, full of food that dogs would love to eat. I would have liked to slow down and sniff every shelf, but nobody here seemed to like dogs at all, and the angry men were close behind me.

Now I was back to a familiar place. The rack full of chickens was right ahead of me.

I rushed past it. A woman with a sack in her arms was strolling toward the glass doors, and they slid open for her.

"No!" somebody howled.

I knew that word, but it was clearly not about me. I was doing the only thing I could possibly do—getting out of this place as soon as I could!—so nobody should be shouting *no* at me.

The woman with the sack in her arms, though, stopped and turned, so perhaps the *no* was about her. I raced right past her, brushing her legs, and out into the night.

The sitting man was still by the wall, laughing as I tore past. "Go, Bella!" he shouted after me.

I heard my name, but I didn't stop. I loped into the darkness, putting the wonderful food building

behind me, and headed down a street with houses and yards.

After I had gone a few blocks, I paused, panting. I heard a dog challenge me from behind a fence, so I knew I was in a safe place now, a place that *liked* dogs. I dropped the chicken to the ground and settled down on my belly to crunch through the rest of my dinner.

When I awoke, I felt warm sun on my back. I had noticed the days growing hotter and hotter, but this was the warmest I had felt yet.

I yawned and stretched and got to my feet, glancing around me. I still felt anxious, as if I had been a bad dog. Maybe the angry men were still looking for me. I stayed away from people that day, moving cautiously between houses, sniffing hopefully at plastic bins with food smells hidden inside. I could not find any bins with an open lid, but I did knock over one that spilled out a pile of soft noodles in a cheesy sauce.

Later, as the sky started to darken again, I passed a garage with a door that was not closed all the way. A gap just wide enough for me was left between the door and the floor, and a smell that I recognized drifted through that gap.

Dog food!

I squeezed into the garage and nosed around until I found a bag of dog food, mostly full, in a corner. I

ripped it open and ate eagerly. I was not being a bad dog now; I was sure of that. Dog food was for dogs!

There were two other dogs on the other side of a door who did not agree that I was doing what a good dog should. They howled and barked and scrabbled at the door with their claws. But I ignored them as I crunched and gulped.

Eating dog food reminded me of Lucas. I remembered how excited I felt when he would take down the dog food from a cupboard and pour it into a bowl. I would dance around the kitchen, too happy to stay still. How grateful I felt. How much I loved Lucas, my very own person, giving me food with his hand.

Homesickness gripped me, as powerful as hunger. As soon as I'd finished this meal, I would leave this town. I would do Go Home to Lucas.

I would head back up into the mountains.

21

I had been doing Go Home for such a long time that everything about it was familiar—the trails through the hills, the search for water, the smell of animals, the lack of food. Days went past, and I headed steadily toward Go Home.

Once I startled a rabbit, but they had not gotten any easier to catch. Once I crept down to a road and found some old hot dog pieces in a metal bin that I knocked over. Other than that, I was not doing very well at feeding myself.

Dogs are not supposed to feed themselves. That's why there are people.

After I gobbled up the hot dogs, I lifted my nose to the breeze. The hair along my back stirred as I caught a new scent. At least three of the small bad dogs were nearby.

I did not want to meet them, so I headed back into the woods, moving uphill. The odor faded behind me.

Then, as I crossed a small stream and drank my fill, I picked up their scent again. It was so strong I turned and stared down the slope behind me, expecting to see them slink out from behind some rocks or trees.

I did not see them, but I could tell they were close.

I was being hunted.

I headed up along the trail again, because there was nowhere else to go. Soon I saw the glow of unfiltered sunlight ahead. The trail burst from the trees and into a large stretch of grassy meadow. There was nowhere to hide here. The small bad dogs would see me easily.

Far ahead, the meadow sloped steeply upward. I could see a jumble of boulders poking up through the grass. The wind was behind me, blowing my scent uphill toward those boulders, but nothing leaped out to run me down. There were no bad dogs there waiting for me.

I remembered the last time I'd been threatened by the small dogs. A good dog learns when things repeat. Last time, having the rock wall behind me had protected me and frustrated my attackers. If I could reach those large boulders now, I would have a chance.

My legs were weak and tired from so many days without good food. Even so, I began running uphill.

I could feel the pack of predators behind me. They were closing in.

I was panting hard when I reached the rocks, and

I lay in a small pool of shade for a time to catch my breath. From here, I could see the entire meadow below me. I spotted the small dogs when they trotted out from the woods.

Single file, they advanced through the grass toward me.

My lips drew back in a snarl.

I was not thinking about Lucas for that moment. I did not feel the pull of Go Home.

All I wanted was to face my enemies, to sink my teeth into their flesh. I got to my feet, ready for the fight to begin.

My three enemies climbed up the hill silently. Their tongues hung out. Their eyes were slits.

As they grew near they spread out, since they knew that I could not retreat. The rocks behind me held me in place.

I could smell that they were a family, all young males from the same litter. I could smell that they were hungry. In fact, they were starving. I was bigger than any of them, but they were desperate. They would not give up easily.

And if they knew how to hunt as a pack, they would win.

I longed to lunge at them, to chase them away, but I stayed with my tail to the boulders. I barked, snapping my teeth, warning them. They drew back, nosing each other. I saw that they were accustomed to prey that fled. Prey that fought back was new to them.

One of them, a bit bigger than his brothers, darted ahead. I jumped forward to meet him. He danced back and his two brothers moved to the side together, instead of flanking me on each side. They did know how to hunt as a pack. I turned to face them and sensed the largest one leaping at me. I snarled and snapped at him and the two smaller ones charged.

I chopped the air with my fangs, knocking over a small dog, and the bold one took his turn to spring. I felt teeth on my neck, tearing my flesh. I screamed and twisted and slashed and bit, and we went up on our back legs. I forced him down with my heavier weight, but one of his brothers darted forward.

Then there was a blur of motion above me. Something had climbed up on the boulders behind me and jumped, soaring over my head and landing right in front of the small bad dogs.

The pack was snarling and yelping in shock and fear. They scrambled back. I stared in amazement as an enormous cat, far larger than I was, sprang at the nearest bad dog, claws slashing. Her massive paw struck the boldest dog on his haunches and sent him tumbling.

The scent of the giant feline filled my senses, and I wagged. I knew this cat. It was Big Kitten.

And she had grown into a very, very *Big* Kitten!

The three bad dogs were fleeing down the hill in a panic. Big Kitten loped easily after them for a moment before she turned to look at me.

I wagged.

She came to me and purred and rubbed her head under my chin, nearly knocking me over. I play bowed, and she knew what to do. She put out one enormous paw and swatted at my nose, keeping her sharp claws in. I dodged away and darted back to put my paws on her shoulders, just as I used to do when we played. But I had to jump up to do it, lifting my front feet off the ground.

When she turned and headed uphill, I followed. She was my pack. She led me to the carcass of an elk, half-buried in shallow dirt. We fed side by side, as we had done so many times before.

Once my stomach was full, I lay down in a patch of sunny grass. I was tired. Big Kitten came over and licked at the wound in my neck, her rough tongue scrubbing at my skin until I turned away from her with a sigh.

She went away in the night, but I stayed where I lay, sleeping curled up in the grass. As the sun was rising, she returned, settling down next to me and purring.

I rested with her, resisting the urge to get up, to get moving, to do Go Home. This was part of our pattern, our way of being a pack. We would stay with the elk carcass for a few days and eat as much as possible before we moved on.

We would do this until we were with Lucas, and then we would not need to hunt any longer.

I wondered if Big Kitten would sleep on the bed with Lucas and me or across the street with Mother Cat.

Big Kitten did not stay close during the day, but she came to find me at night. Sometimes she led me to a meal, usually buried in the dirt.

Several times I smelled humans in the forest and went to find the spots where they stayed and where they filled up the metal bins with food. I gobbled down small morsels but took big things—chunks of bread, pieces of meat—up to share with Big Kitten.

We were making progress toward Lucas. I could feel it. And the closer we got to Go Home, the stronger its pull became.

We had been a pack again for some time the day we crossed a wide meadow. Other animals had been here before us, and had left large brown piles half hidden in the short, dry grass. I could see and smell that these big piles did not come from dogs. I sniffed them with interest and even licked one, but I could not figure out who had left them behind.

In the middle of the field was a strange kind of car or truck. It had four wooden wheels that had sunk halfway into the dirt, and a flat wooden frame between them that was half rotted away. I examined it with a little wariness, since things with wheels were often connected with humans. But I could smell that no people had been around this object for a very long time.

The sky was beginning to darken overhead, so I crawled underneath the wooden surface, resting in the shady dirt between the wheels. It was a comfortable

spot for the night. Big Kitten would find me here after a while, and we would sleep together.

I dozed off.

In the morning, when I woke, I could not feel Big Kitten's warmth against me. I could not smell her nearby.

But I could smell other animals. Lots of them.

I looked out from under my wooden shelter, and I saw feet. Many, many feet. They were very odd feet, too—not like dog feet, with our sturdy pads, or like cat feet with their sharp claws that can slide in and out. These feet were hard and round, with a crack down the middle that split them into two halves.

Cautiously I wiggled out from my sleeping spot. I could not believe what I saw and smelled.

There were animals all around me—huge animals, much taller than I was. They had the strange feet I had seen already, and long legs, and huge, *huge* bodies covered in dense, curly hair, much thicker than the fur of any dog I had ever seen.

Their heads were the size of my body and were crowned with curved horns that came to sharp points. Some of these heads bobbed down to the grass and nibbled at it. Other heads turned to look at me curiously. One of the creatures twitched its tail out of the way and let loose an enormous *plop!* down in the grass, and I realized that these were the animals who had left the piles that I'd encountered yesterday.

I had gotten used to being one of the biggest ani-

mals around. I was bigger than most dogs (well, except Dutch). I had once been bigger than Big Kitten, although that was not true anymore. I was bigger than the rabbits and squirrels I chased, bigger than the bad dogs who'd tried to hunt me twice. But these animals made me feel tiny. I could smell that they were not hunters—they did not eat other creatures, just plants. But I did not want to be near them.

One of them, smaller than the rest, seemed curious about me. It moved away from the side of a larger one and took several clopping steps in my direction.

I took a few steps backward.

It stretched out its nose toward me and made a strange grunting bleat.

That was all I needed to hear! I turned and leaped away, running through the crowd around me, darting around those huge, hard feet and dodging horned heads that swiveled to stare at me.

Soon I was away and could put on more speed as I headed up a hill along the side of the meadow. Behind me, the big creatures returned to their grazing. Dogs did not seem to matter to them.

The hill was not steep, but it was long. I panted as I toiled up the slope. I was nearly at the top when I caught a familiar smell and put on a little extra speed.

Big Kitten was waiting for me. She had settled down on top of a boulder, basking sleepily in the sun. I supposed she had not come to sleep with me under the thing with wheels because she had not liked the big

animals, either. Or maybe because their smell had masked mine, and she had not been able to find me.

I touched noses with her, and she rubbed her face on mine. I jumped up to the boulder beside her. Now I could see the herd of big creatures on one side of the hill below us. Down the other side of the hill was a town.

A huge town.

The smell lifted up toward my nose, and I realized where we were.

We had found Go Home.

22

Excitement flashed through me. I bounded down the slope, but then I realized that I was alone.

I looked back. Big Kitten was sitting on her rock, not moving.

I trotted back to her, wondering why she was not following me. We were a pack and should stay together. Lucas was waiting for us.

She leaped lightly to the ground and rubbed her head against me. Then she scampered back toward the top of the hill. It was as if she wanted to go away from home and down the slope, back toward the meadow with the big animals, back toward the forests and the hills where people hardly ever came.

She looked over her shoulder at me. She wanted me to follow her.

When I didn't move, she returned to me. This time

she didn't rub herself against me. She just sat and stared at me, tucking her tail around her so that it curled around her front paws.

The two of us looked at each other for a while. Then, at last, I felt that I understood.

Big Kitten was not going to do Go Home with me. She would not be lying on Lucas's bed with me, waiting for a T-i-i-ny Piece of Cheese. For some reason, she did not want to go downhill with me toward the town that lay spread out below.

It was as if she wanted to do Go Home herself, as if she had a place where she needed to be. But her Go Home was not the same as mine.

I went to her, wagging, and touched her with my nose. I loved Big Kitten. She was my pack. But now she was large enough to hunt for herself. She did not need me to help her find food or to drive off the small bad dogs if they threatened her.

She did not need me to be her Mother Cat anymore.

So far my life had taught me that I might stay for a while with a family, like Uncle José and Aunt Loretta or Gavin and Taylor. But the time would come to move on, and it was that time now.

I had to do Go Home.

I turned and made my way down the slope toward the big town below. When I looked back, Big Kitten had jumped up on her rock once more. Dutch had been confused and upset when I'd said goodbye, but Big Kitten merely watched as I set off downhill again.

She was still there the next time I glanced back, and the next.

Then I looked again, and Big Kitten was gone.

S teadily, I drew closer to the big town. A sound reached my ears, growing louder minute by minute. It was a steady roaring, and it made me nervous. But to reach the town, I had to get closer to that noise.

Soon I could see what was making such a racket—a road. Cars and trucks were speeding along it, going so fast that the wind they made blasted into my face and made my ears flap.

I had driven on roads like this, when I had done car rides with Lucas and Mom, or with Gavin and Taylor. Car rides were fun—when you were in a car.

Being on the outside of the cars was not fun at all.

But I needed to cross this road. I knew I did. I lay down in a stand of tall grass and waited and waited for the cars to give me some space.

The cars didn't seem to know that I needed to get to Lucas. They kept rushing past. At last I got impatient.

If the cars would not let me go, I'd have to go myself.

I stood up. I tensed. A dark car rushed by, its tires only feet from my nose. Another followed close behind it. Then there was a little space, a gap between that car and the next.

I lunged forward into that gap, running as fast as I could go.

One of the cars made a blaring, honking sound. It skidded to a halt, turning on the road, as I bounded ahead.

A small truck crunched into a low fence made of metal that ran down the middle of the road, separating one half from another. Inside the truck, someone was yelling.

A woman leaped out of the car that had stopped. "Here, pooch!" she called out.

I was afraid she thought I was a bad dog. I ran away from her. She ran, too, following me.

I bunched my legs underneath me and leaped over the metal fence. More cars were on the other side. They made the same honking noises I'd heard before, and their tires screamed on the pavement as they skidded and stopped.

The woman jumped the fence behind me. More people leaped out of their stopped cars. "Here, dog! Here, boy!" some of them called out. "Come! Stay!" other people shouted.

It was very confusing. What did all these people want me to do?

A man jumped in front of me, waving his arms. I dodged away from him with a frightened yip. I didn't want him to grab me. I didn't want any of these people to grab me!

I wanted Lucas!

I was racing past a truck now, and someone flung its door open. A man leaped out. He had a big hat on his head and tall boots that thumped when they hit the pavement.

"I got this!" he shouted.

He grabbed something from inside the truck—a rope! A very long rope. It had a loop in it, and it swung the loop in a big circle above his head.

I ran faster.

The man flung the rope at me, but I knew better than to let something like that touch me. I dodged. The rope hit the roadway with a heavy *smack*.

The cars on the road had all stopped now, as far as I could see. I wondered why, but it certainly made the running easier.

Ahead of me, a woman stepped out of a light-colored van. Other people drew away from her. She had something in her hand—a long metal pole with a wire loop on one end.

In her other hand she held out something that, even in my panic, I could smell. It smelled tasty.

Treats! She was holding treats!

"All right, folks. Animal control! Let me handle this!" she called out.

She came toward me, holding out her hand. "Here, doggie. Want a treat?" she called out. "Good dog. Come!"

I hesitated.

I knew the words this woman was saying—dog, come, treat.

Should I go to her? Was that what a good dog would do?

The woman reached out toward me with her long metal pole. The wire loop came close to my head.

I remembered a pole with a loop like that. When it went over my head, it had been a strange, uncomfortable leash that had taken me on a car ride I did not want.

I knew what to do now. I must get away from the person with this leash. I must not let her touch me, even though she had treats.

I turned and dashed away in the opposite direction, away from the woman, away from her treats and her strange leash. Ahead of me, two cars had parked right next to each other, with the front bumper of the back car stuck deep into the rear bumper of the one in front.

I flung myself under the cars, wiggled on my belly, shoved with my back feet, and burst out on the other side, running as fast as I could go.

Ahead of me was a wooden fence, taller than the metal one I'd jumped over earlier. But I could do it! I could get over this fence, too! I put all my strength into my leap, and I was soaring over it.

I landed hard on stony ground. The thump hurt all over, from my paws to my tail, but I did not have time to worry about that.

I flung myself forward, but I felt a worse pain in one rear paw. It was trapped! My foot had slipped into a crack between two rocks and I could not get it out.

I lunged and tugged at my trapped foot. It hurt so much I whimpered out load.

"Easy, girl. Easy!" called a voice behind me.

The woman with the strange leash was struggling over the fence. She got to her feet and walked slowly toward me, holding her leash out toward my face.

"We don't want you to hurt yourself," she said softly. "Just stay still, girl. Just stay still."

I could not let that strange leash touch me. I could not let this woman take me away. Not now, not when I was finally so close, so very close, to Go Home.

I yanked on my trapped foot with all my strength. The woman jumped forward, trying to get me. But it was too late! I yelped with pain as my foot came loose, and the woman stumbled and fell down on one knee as I raced away, down the stony slope, into a small stand of trees, across a much smaller and quieter road, and away. Away from all these cars and people. Toward the town, toward Lucas, toward Go Home.

My foot hurt every time my weight landed on it, but I did not let that stop me. I would not let anything stop me.

I was very close now. Soon, soon, I could be Go Home.

It was dusk when I limped into the town at last. There were leaves on the ground, scuttling ahead of me in a light breeze.

I knew this town was the right one. I knew it was Go Home.

But where was Lucas?

I slept under a bench in a park that smelled like children and dogs. That night I had strange dreams. I felt Big Kitten's rough tongue on my neck where the small bad dog had bitten me. I felt Gavin and Taylor with their arms around me. Dutch groaned with contentment in my ear. I tasted Uncle José's salty treats and felt Aunt Loretta arrange my Lucas blanket around me.

It was as if they had all come to tell me goodbye.

In the morning I woke and shook myself alert. My foot hurt less today, and I could put more weight on it. I found a clear, cold river and drank from it eagerly.

People walked along a path by the river, and some of them even had dogs on leashes, but I stayed away from them. I had no way to know which ones might try to keep me from getting to Lucas. And I was so close now. I could not let anyone slow me down.

Behind some buildings I found a bin so overstuffed that the lid was propped open. I tried to knock it over, but had no luck. So I leaped up and thrust my snout under the lip, grabbing at the first thing I touched. It was a sack with nothing to eat inside it. I tried again, and this time I snagged a plastic bag with chicken in it, and also a foil wrapping that had spicy meat and flat bread.

After I ate I lifted my nose to the air, sniffing carefully. I could smell people, many people. I could smell

cars with their combination of metal and smoke and rubber. I could smell squirrels and cats and dogs and clean snow high up in the mountains.

Somewhere among all these smells was my boy.

I trotted forward, keeping my nose high into the breeze. The smell of Go Home was starting to separate itself into distinct parts. It was the opposite of what had happened when Audrey drove me away from Lucas. Then, trees and dirt and people and water and houses had all blurred together into one single smell. Now each part of that smell was becoming itself again.

My legs were getting tired, but when I reached the park where Lucas used to throw the ball up the slide, new energy surged through me. I bounded forward. Children were swinging on the swings and sliding down the slide, and two female dogs raced forward to sniff me. I let them investigate the spot beneath my tail, just to be polite, but I could not stop and play.

I was almost Go Home.

23

Now I ran through the grass, across several streets (one car made a long honking bark at me, but I ignored it), and turned one last corner. Everything around me was familiar now—each tree, each bush, each square of the sidewalk. My nose knew everything I met.

Except for one thing.

The house where I had been born, where I had lived with my family and with Mother Cat, was not there. A tall building had taken its place. I could smell many people inside, their scents flowing out of open windows.

But I had no time to investigate this new building. I was almost there! I had done Go Home!

I dashed along the sidewalk to my very own porch. I knew I should curl up behind the chair, but it was missing and anyway I was too impatient to be a good

dog. I jumped up on my back legs to scratch at the door, wagging and barking. This was no moment for No Barks. Lucas would open the door now. Lucas!

The door opened. A woman I had never met stood there. Home smells poured out around her. "Hello, dear," she said to me.

I wagged, but she was not Lucas. I pushed past her into the house.

"Oh, my!" she said behind me, but I did not pay attention.

I could not smell Lucas. I could not smell Mom.

There was a new couch in the living room instead of the one where Mom had lain so often. The table was different. Lucas's room did not have a bed in it.

"What are you doing, sweetheart?" the strange new woman asked when I came back out of Lucas's room and joined her in the kitchen. "Are you looking for something?" She held out a hand to me.

I went to her, wagging. Could she explain somehow? Where was Lucas?

People can do wonderful things, like open doors and fill bowls with food and make cars go for rides and find toys that have vanished under the furniture. I was hoping that this person could fix this problem for me, because it was clearly not something a dog could understand.

"Whoever you're looking for isn't here, sweetie," the woman said to me.

I couldn't understand her words, but I could tell she was not going to help me.

I felt sick inside.

Lucas was gone.

I needed to go outside, to get moving once more. I had not done Go Home right, because Lucas was not here. The point of Go Home was to be where Lucas was.

I went to the door and sat, waiting for the woman to open it.

She came over to me and very gently took my chin in her palm. She looked at me carefully. "I have the sense that you came here for a very important reason," she told me. "But I don't have anything to do with it, do I?"

I heard the kindness in her voice and wagged.

"I hope you find what you're looking for," she told me, and she opened the door.

I dashed outside. But where should I go?

For so long, I had been doing Go Home. I had known exactly what to do. Even when it had been hard and lonely and hungry, I had kept on. I'd found my way to the right town and the right street and the right door.

But not the right person.

What should I do now? Where should I go? I roamed restlessly along the street, moving from yard to yard. I could not stay still, because I was not Go Home. But I didn't know where to find it anymore.

I moved through yards with swings and slides, yards with bushes, yards with trees. Sometimes a person came to a doorway and spoke to me, or someone on a sidewalk held out a hand.

I ignored them. They were not the right person. There was only one right person—Lucas.

Where had he gone?

As I crossed yet another yard, a familiar scent drifted up from the grass at my feet. I put my nose down and sniffed. It had been a long time since I'd had that smell in my nose, but I knew it at once.

I followed the smell to a space underneath a deck. There were thin strips of wood that kept me from crawling into the darkness under there, but in one spot there was a hollow in the dirt where something small could squirm beneath the slats. I put my nose into the hollow and whined.

Mother Cat was underneath there. I could smell her. She had found herself a new den.

I pulled my head back and waited. In a moment she came out, purring, and stretched up to rub her head against my chin.

She was plumper than she had been when we'd lived together in our old den, and her fur was smoother. But even so, she was so tiny! I did not know how she had gotten herself so small.

I was still anxious to find Lucas, but the touch and smell of my cat mother was a comfort to me. She had been my second family, and right now she was the only family I could find.

Mother Cat leapt gracefully up onto the railing of the deck and balanced there, looking down at me. I found some steps so that I could climb up to be with her.

Now that we were on top of the deck, I could see that it was connected to a house. There was a door made entirely of glass, and near it were a bowl of water and another one with food in it. The smell of humans was on both bowls. I realized that someone was taking care of my mother here at her new den, just as Lucas had fed her at the old one.

Mother Cat sat and watched me as I gobbled up the moist, fishy food in her bowl. There was not much there, but the few bites I gulped down were delicious. She licked my face after I'd finished. I licked her back, politely, and left her entire head damp from my tongue.

Then the glass door slid open. A woman stood there. She smelled of flour and sugar. I expected my cat mother to run, but she didn't. Instead, she went and sat by the bowl, looking up at the woman expectantly.

Maybe there would be more food soon? I did Sit, too.

"Daisy? Who is this dog?" the woman asked.

I wagged at the word *dog*.

"Oh, Daisy, this is a stray. She doesn't even have a collar. Did she eat your food?" The woman frowned at me. "Shoo, dog. You don't belong here."

The woman pointed. She moved her hand quickly through the air, as if she were throwing a ball. I turned my head, but I didn't see a ball hit the ground. I looked back at the woman.

"Go home!" she told me.

I jumped to my feet, suddenly anxious. I had *done* Go Home! It hadn't worked!

"Go!" the woman shouted.

I could see that she thought I was a bad dog, maybe because I hadn't done Go Home the way I should have. I slunk off the deck back down to the grass. Mother Cat followed me.

"Daisy? Kitty-kitty?" the woman called after her. "Daisy, come here!"

Cats don't understand the word *come*. I had noticed that before. Mother Cat did not go toward the woman who had called out *come*. Instead, she followed me to the next yard, where I found a spot under the bushes to curl up.

Mother Cat curled up with me and purred, which was comforting. But I still missed Lucas. And I still did not know how to do Go Home anymore.

In the morning Mother Cat got up and stretched in the grass. I did the same. She trotted off in a new direction, and since I did not know what else to do, I followed her.

She did not take me back to the deck where there had been food in a bowl. Instead, she took me to another house. This one had a patio of hard brick near the back door. Mother Cat sat beside the door and it opened up. I stayed a little way back, in case the person who opened this door would think I was a bad dog, too.

"There you are, Princess, right on time," a man said. He put down a bowl and shut the door.

Mother Cat put her head down to the bowl. I moved forward and did the same thing. We shared, just like

we had done long ago, in the den under the house, before I became Lucas's dog.

Then Mother Cat led me to a different house. This time nobody came to the door, but there was crunchy food in a bowl on the front porch.

This reminded me of the times I had led Big Kitten through the wilderness and we had stopped at all those places with the metal bins full of food. I had led Big Kitten to food then, and Mother Cat was doing the same thing for me now.

Also, I was beginning to see why Mother Cat was not skinny any longer.

At the next house, there was another deck. A woman was sitting at a small table with a mug of something hot in her hand. Mother Cat jumped up and I found some stairs, just as I had before. I climbed up the stairs carefully, checking to see if the woman would tell me to Go Home or pretend to throw a ball.

"Molly, did you find a friend?" the woman asked. She did not get up as I followed Mother Cat to a bowl of damp food that tasted a little bit like chicken. Mother Cat had three bites and I had the rest.

"Hmmm. You look very hungry," the woman said quietly.

She got up, moving slowly. I backed away, in case she would think I was a bad dog because I wasn't doing Go Home. But she didn't seem to think so. She just opened a door and went inside, leaving the door open behind her.

"Want some more?" she called out.

I heard a can being opened. I heard food plopping into a bowl. These were very good sounds.

Mother Cat thought so, too, because she went to the door and looked in. I peered over her head. The woman had put a bowl with more food in it on the floor of a kitchen.

"Come on in," she told me.

Food! I trotted in and gulped down everything in the bowl. Then I turned back to look at Mother Cat in the doorway.

"Molly never comes inside," the woman told me. "She's been a stray a long time. She's nervous around people. You, though—you're not nervous at all, are you?" Slowly, she reached out to me and scratched my neck. Her hands smelled like chicken. I licked them and let her pet me. It felt good to have human attention, even if the person giving me the attention wasn't Lucas.

"What a sweet dog!" the woman said. "But no collar, huh? I think you need some help, baby."

Still moving slowly, she got up and shut the door.

24

I trotted over to the closed door and scratched at it with one paw. Mother Cat was out there. I wanted to be with her.

I looked up at Chicken Lady. She could open the door for me. People know how to do things like that.

But she didn't. She did give me some more chicken, though, and a bowl full of water.

"So there's a really big dog in our kitchen," a new voice said while I was lapping. I looked up. Another woman was in the doorway, wearing pajamas. She had bare feet.

I gulped down another drink and went to sniff at her feet. She shuffled back.

"It's okay. She's so friendly," said Chicken Lady.

"You think all dogs are friendly," Pajama Lady said.

She reached out a hand to stroke my head lightly. "Sheesh, she's filthy."

"I know. She's a stray."

I was licking Pajama Lady's toes. They had an interesting taste.

Pajama Lady giggled. "Okay, I admit that she's probably not dangerous. But we can't keep her! You know we can't have pets in this place. You're not even supposed to be feeding that cat."

"I know."

"So you're going to call animal control?"

Chicken Lady picked up her phone and, after a moment, talked into it.

Pajama Lady cooked some eggs and ate them and gave me some. Then she cooked some more, just for me, setting them on the floor on a plate. "Well, she looks so hungry," she said defensively to Chicken Lady.

Then Pajama Lady put on different clothes and shoes and rushed around picking up things, like a purse and a phone and some jingling keys. She hurried out of the house. Chicken Lady talked on the phone some more and then sat on the floor and talked to me.

I went to the door a few more times and whined and scratched at it, but she didn't get the hint.

After a while, someone knocked at the front door. I did No Barks, but I didn't get a treat. Chicken Lady went to the door and opened it. I stayed in the kitchen, sniffing at the floor to investigate all the food smells.

The front door opened. I heard voices talking. A familiar smell gusted into the house and rolled over me.

I knew that smell! I barreled out of the kitchen, heading straight for the new arrivals.

Audrey stood at the door, talking to Chicken Lady. Olivia walked inside. Chicken Lady shut the door behind her.

All of them turned to stare at me as I raced out of the kitchen. Chicken Lady let out a yelp of surprise. Audrey spread her hands wide, ready to grab me.

I skidded to a stop at Olivia's feet and jumped up to put my front paws on her. Olivia sat down hard on the floor of the hallway.

It had been so long since I'd met a person I knew!

Maybe I'd done Go Home right after all? At least a little?

I was licking Olivia's face, nuzzling my nose into her neck, and sniffing up all her good smells. "It's okay, Mom. It's okay! She's friendly!" Olivia kept saying.

Olivia had a light jacket on over her T-shirt. I stuck my nose inside the jacket. It smelled warm and cozy, and I caught a faint scent on the lining.

It smelled like Lucas! Olivia had been near Lucas!

This was so marvelous that I flung myself away from Olivia and raced back to the kitchen and turned around and ran to the hallway again. Olivia had climbed to her feet. I ran into a living room where I skidded on a rug and leaped onto a couch and off it

again before I tumbled back into the hallway and sat at Olivia's feet, panting happily up at her.

"Mom," Olivia said. "Mom. I think . . . you know who I think this is?"

Olivia knelt down beside me, looking carefully at my face.

"Bella?" she said. "You can't be . . . Bella? Is it you?"

"Can't be," Audrey murmured.

I had not heard a human voice saying my name in a long time. It was wonderful! I jumped on Olivia to show how happy I was, and we fell together onto the floor and rolled around there as I wagged and licked wherever I could reach her skin and whined with happiness.

"It is, Mom! It is!" Olivia shouted from underneath me. "It's Bella! She came home!"

After Olivia and I were done being so happy together, and after I'd greeted Audrey, too, and licked Chicken Lady's hands some more, the people all did a lot of talking and calling on their phones. Audrey had brought a collar and a leash, and she put them on me. "Bella, Bella, I can't believe it's you!" she kept saying.

Then we took a car ride, Audrey and Olivia and me. Chicken Lady did not get to come. Audrey drove, and Olivia sat in the back seat with me.

"I still can't believe it, Bella," she told me. "We searched so hard for you! Mom, do you think she *walked* home?"

"Maybe she did," Audrey said. "She looks like it."

Olivia sniffed. "And she smells like it, too. Whew, girl, you stink! Are we there yet, Mom?"

"Ten more minutes," Audrey said from the front seat.

We'd left the scent of Go Home far behind us, which made me a little nervous. We were driving through fields with trees in the distance, and I could smell in the air rushing through the windows that we were coming up on a different town, a new one.

Should we be leaving Go Home like this? Of course Audrey and Olivia were not the kind of people who would try to keep me from Lucas . . . except that they had done so, long ago. The last time I'd gone on a car ride with them, we'd gone to Uncle José and Aunt Loretta's house, and Lucas had not been there. That had been the start of this whole long journey.

I moved away from Olivia. I stuck my nose out of the other window, searching for familiar odors. I whined.

"It's okay, girl. It's okay, Bella. You're going to be so happy so soon!" Olivia told me.

At last the car stopped moving. We were parked in a driveway, and a small house was next to it.

"Did you text him?" asked Olivia as Audrey pulled the keys from the lot.

"Of course I did. Keep hold of the leash when you open the door. She's agitated," Audrey said.

Olivia picked up the leash and opened the car door. I jumped out and lifted my nose to the air. Did I have to start Go Home all over again?

The smell that rushed into my nose was over-whelming. Lucas was here! This driveway, this lawn, this house was full of his smell.

Then the door of the house opened and he was there.

My boy. My person.

Lucas.

I pulled the leash right out of Olivia's hand, and Lucas and I ran to each other. We met on the front lawn and fell to the ground together. I climbed on him and lay down right on top of him, licking his face and his neck and his hands. "Bella! Bella!" Lucas kept saying.

I had done Go Home. I was Go Home with Lucas.

He pushed me off a little bit so he could sit up. I was yipping, not doing No Barks, and I ran in a circle around him and threw myself into his lap. Mom came out of the house, too. She did not have her stick with her now, although she still walked with a limp. She came to us and kneeled down beside us both. "It's actually her," she said in amazement.

"Bella. Bella, we looked so hard for you!" Lucas told me. He took my face in both hands. "You're so skinny. Look how skinny she is!"

"I think she came on a very long journey to find you," Mom said, reaching out to pet me, too. Olivia knelt down on the other side of Lucas, and I wiggled onto my back in Lucas's lap so that she could rub my tummy.

I had never felt so loved. Olivia leaned over and kissed Lucas on the check, and he kissed her back. They were doing love, too.

That's what Go Home meant. It was love. And I had done it at last.

After that there was more food for me, which was wonderful, and a bath, which was not. And then there was the best thing ever—a bed with a blanket on it. My Lucas blanket!

I flopped down on the bed and lay there happily. Lucas lay beside me, and Olivia sat cross-legged next to us. Mom looked in the door and then limped away, smiling.

Lucas rubbed my neck. "There's a scar here. I can't imagine what she went through."

"Mom says it's four hundred miles from Aunt Loretta and Uncle José's house to your old place," Olivia said. "By the roads. She doesn't know how long if you try to walk through the mountains. Do you really think she did that, Lucas?"

I wagged sleepily for Lucas's name.

"Yeah, I think she did. But I don't know how she survived. How could she have found enough to eat?" Lucas sat up on the bed. "Wait! I just thought of something!" He jumped off the bed and ran out of the room.

I sat up, ready to run after him, but he was back in a moment, holding something small in his hand.

I could smell what it was. I went on high alert, my whole body rigid, waiting.

"It's such a tiny piece of cheese!" Olivia said, giggling.

Yes! T-i-i-ny Piece of Cheese!

"I know, but she loves it. Watch her stare at it." Lucas brought his hand slowly up, then down, then close to my face. Closer . . . closer . . .

At last the cheese was close enough. Gently, I removed it from his fingers. The explosion of taste on my tongue lasted only a moment, but it was exactly what I had been longing for all this time: a treat, hand-fed to me by my person.

Lucas flopped on the bed again and I lay close beside him. I thought back to my hungry days on the trail, when all I could think about was my T-i-i-ny Piece of Cheese. It was just as wonderful as I remembered.

I lay there, thinking about how hungry I had been for so long. I thought of Big Kitten, how she sat and watched me from the rocks where I'd last seen her. I had taken care of Big Kitten when she needed me. I hoped she was doing well now that I was not there to look after her.

Just as I'd taken care of Big Kitten, others had taken care of me. Gavin and Taylor had loved me. So had Uncle José and Aunt Loretta. And I had loved them, too, but I could not stay with them. I needed to find Lucas. I knew they would understand.

Now, curled up with Lucas and Olivia, I was back with my people and would never leave again. I was a good dog.

Finally, finally, I was Go Home.

Reading & Activity Guide to

Bella's Story

By W. Bruce Cameron

Ages 8–12; Grades 3–7

Loyal, loving pit-bull mix Bella forms an unbreakable bond with Lucas, after the determined thirteen-year-old boy rescues her from a house earmarked for demolition. Basking in his attention, reciprocating his affection, and helping Lucas support his wounded, military-veteran mother become Bella's defining missions. But her black-and-white view of the world and her place in it is turned upside-down when a meddlesome neighbor contacts animal control. According to the local law, if animal control sees a pit-bull-breed dog like Bella off of Lucas's property, they can take her away and even euthanize her. To keep her safe until he and his mother can relocate to a place that allows pit bulls, Lucas reluctantly agrees to send Bella to stay with a friend's aunt and uncle in a town over four hundred miles away. Confused by the separation and determined to reunite with her beloved Lucas, Bella escapes and embarks on an arduous journey through mountainous terrain. In *Bella's Story*, readers get a dog's-eye view of bittersweet adventures, harrowing encounters, and invaluable life lessons as Bella faithfully discharges her most important duty: to "Go Home."

Reading *Bella's Story* with Your Children

Pre-Reading Discussion Questions

1. *Bella's Story* is based on W. Bruce Cameron's adult novel *A Dog's Way Home,* which was made into a major motion picture. W. Bruce Cameron also wrote *Shelby's Story,* imagining the fictionalized back story of Shelby, the animal actor who played Bella in the *A Dog's Way Home* movie. Have you read or seen any of these other works? If so, how does that affect your ideas about, or expectations of, *Bella's Story* or its canine main character? In cases where there is a book and a movie of the same story, which you do you prefer to check out first—the book or the movie? Why?

2. If you haven't read or seen the other works (novel, chapter book, or movie) related to the character of Bella, can you think of a movie or book you enjoyed that featured a dog or other animal as the main character? What was interesting or appealing about that animal character?

3. *Bella's Story* imagines an amazing journey a devoted pet makes to reunite with her owner. Have you heard or read a nonfiction story in which a pet or animal did something heroic or unusual to help their owner? What were the circumstances in that story?

Post-Reading Discussion Questions

1. In Chapter 1, we meet the book's canine narrator, Bella. Although she is a stray pup sheltering in a crawl space, her "voice" is optimistic. Can you think

of some examples from her descriptions of her home, family, and (feline) neighbors that illustrate her positive attitude?

2. When people with blazing flashlights invade the crawl space, Bella observes: "These were the first humans I had ever seen. Even though the light and the noises were alarming, something deep inside me was interested, too. I almost wanted to run toward the people as they crawled into the den." Can you think of other examples from *Bella's Story* where Bella experiences mixed feelings about people, or their actions or intentions?

3. In Chapter 2, Lucas makes the risky choice to run in front of the bulldozer and demand the demolition workers stop until the remaining animals are rescued. Do you think this was the right choice? If you were in Lucas's position, would you have done the same thing? Why or why not?

4. Author W. Bruce Cameron emphasizes rich, sensory details, and uses techniques like personification (assigning human qualities or actions to inanimate objects) to create an authentic, dog's-eye point of view in *Bella's Story*. Lacking a frame of reference for what a bulldozer is or does, for example, Bella comments: "The big square thing stopped moving. It stopped growling too." How does the author's use of personification and sensory-driven descriptions help convey how human objects and activities, and even humans themselves, appear from Bella's perspective?

5. Several of the story's key human characters make decisions in Chapter 3 that significantly impact what

happens next both for Bella and the story. Olivia doesn't tell her mother (rescue-worker Audrey) that Lucas has Bella. Audrey realizes it's Bella, not a "baseball mitt," in Lucas's jacket, but doesn't insist on taking the puppy back to the rescue. And Lucas decides that he is going to keep Bella and bring her home without asking for his mother's permission first. Do you agree or disagree with each of these decisions? Why or why not? Explain your answers.

6. What do we learn about Lucas and his mom's relationship, and circumstances, through their discussion in Chapter 4 about Lucas keeping Bella?

7. What are some of the special treats and activities that Lucas and Bella share? How does Olivia help Lucas train Bella?

8. In Chapter 5, why do you think the animal control officer decides to give Lucas and Bella a second chance, after the officer initially says it's illegal to have a pit bull within city limits and he's going to have to take Bella? What advice does the animal control officer give Lucas to keep Bella safe? What does Lucas think of the suggestion?

9. In Chapter 6, while the people are talking about the unfairness of the laws against pit bulls, which is a pretty serious and immediate concern, Bella goes over to Lucas, observing: "I went over and put my head in his lap so that he'd remember everything was okay and also that I hadn't had a cookie yet." Do you like it when the author uses humor, through the voice of Bella, to break up tense situations or scenes? Can you think of other examples from the story where

one of Bella's humorous descriptions or observations lightens a stressful moment in the action?

10. In Chapter 7, after she gets her new job, Lucas's mom tells Bella: "Thank you for forcing me to quit making excuses. I thought it would be too hard for me, but I love having a purpose in the world beyond just healing myself. You gave me that. I love you." What role did Bella play in inspiring Lucas's mom to take such positive steps in her life and recovery?

11. When Lucas is saying goodbye to Bella before she is taken to her temporary home with Olivia's aunt and uncle, Lucas says: "But I'm not abandoning you, Bella. I'll come and get you. It won't be long before you can go home." Why is this one of the most pivotal moments in the story? Explain your answer.

12. Why is the timing of Bella's escape from Aunt Loretta and Uncle José's backyard unlucky, or ironic?

13. Why does Bella feel that she needs to take care of Big Kitten when she meets her in Chapter 12? What are some examples, in Chapters 13 and 14, of how Bella's wilder instincts come out?

14. How does Bella help fellow dog Dutch? Why does Dutch being with Gavin and Taylor make it easier for Bella to separate from them?

15. How does Big Kitten defending Bella from the coyotes in Chapter 21 bring their special relationship "full circle"? When Mother Cat helps Bella out (after Bella discovers Lucas and his mom have moved), does that relationship come "full circle" in a way as well? In the last chapter, when Bella is reunited with Lucas at last, does it feel like this central relationship

in the story also represents a circle, or cycle, of love and kindness?

Post-Reading Activities
Take the story from the page to the pavement with these fun and inspiring activities for the dog lovers in your family.

1. **Can you teach an old dog new tricks?**
   Throughout Bella's story, Lucas and others teach Bella basic commands like "Sit" and "Come," as well as more challenging skills like "No Barks" and "Go Home." Using the repetition, reward, and treat strategy modeled in the book, can you teach your family pet (or work with a friend or relative to teach their pet) a new trick, or series of tricks? Consider inviting friends to do the same, and work together to organize a dog show where you and your furry "students" can share the results with an audience of pet-loving family and friends.

2. **Stories with a happy *friend*ing!**
   In *Bella's Story,* animals—sometimes even of different species—lend each other a hand (or a paw!) in difficult circumstances. Think of puppy Bella and Mother Cat; Bella and Big Kitten; Bella and Dutch; or the "pack" of neighborhood dogs, who show Bella where to get food around town. Together with your child, can you research online or at the library stories about unique animal friendships, which developed at zoos, animal sanctuaries, farms, or in the aftermath of a forest fire or natural disaster? If desired, do

an art project together to illustrate one of the special animal friendships you discover. You could make a collage with images and quotes; drawings; paintings; a diorama; or air-dry clay sculptures.

3. **How can *you* help animals in need?**
    Bella's Story examines some of the challenges stray or lost animals can face, as they search for food, water, shelter, and companionship. Animal shelters and rescue organizations do important work to help these animals in need. Consider partnering with your kids to research needs and opportunities you might be able to help out with at your local animal shelters, or rescue organizations.

Reading *Bella's Story* In Your Classroom

These Common Core–aligned writing activities may be used in conjunction with the pre- and post-reading discussion questions above.

1. **Point of View.**
    Bella's Story is narrated by determined pit-bull mix Bella, who won't let anything come between her and the boy she loves. Bella encounters other human and animal characters, who help or hinder her as she finds her way back to Lucas. Big Kitten, for example, becomes a critical friend and ally to Bella, but we only hear about the relationship from Bella's perspective. How might it be different if Big Kitten was describing the friendship? Write two to three

paragraphs from Big Kitten's point of view. Include Big Kitten's first impressions of Bella; what she learns from Bella, and what Bella teaches her; how their friendship develops; and how they make their differences (for example, sleeping habits, desire to avoid or approach people, preference for isolated versus populated areas, playing, feeding, and hunting behaviors) benefits, instead of barriers, in their friendship.

2. **A Family Tale.**

In a one-page essay, discuss how the concept of family is explored throughout *Bella's Story*. What does Bella learn, and experience, about the meaning of family? Does one specific set of biological factors, or specific features, define a family, or is it a more fluid and flexible concept? Can you be part of a temporary family, and "carry" the love and memory of that family with you, even if you become part of another family group? In your essay, you can focus on one family or "pack" from the story, or examine several different scenarios. Use examples and details from the text, as you explore how families or packs in the story formed, functioned, changed, or grew. You can consider human or animal families, or families made up of both. (Some family "models" you might consider could include: Puppy Bella and her littermates and mother dog; the cat and kitten families in Bella's puppyhood "den"; Bella's adoptive family with Mother Cat; Lucas and his mom; Lucas, his mom, and Bella; Aunt Loretta, Uncle José, and Bella; Bella and Big Kitten; and Gavin, Taylor, Dutch, and Bella.)

3. **Text Type: Opinion Piece.**

    In *Bella's Story,* Lucas's neighbor chooses to report Bella to animal control, because Bella is a pit-bull mix. Although Bella herself does not exhibit any aggressive behaviors, pit bulls have a reputation for being dangerous. Some areas (like the place where Lucas lives) have laws forbidding pit bulls, or requiring the dogs be confined to the owners' private property, which can make it difficult to exercise and socialize a pet. In *Bella's Story,* the animal control officer decides to give Lucas a second chance with Bella, even though it's breaking the rules and may put his job in jeopardy. What is *your* opinion? Do you agree with the neighbor who reports Bella and wants her removed from the neighborhood immediately? Or do you agree with the animal control officer, who decides to give Bella and Lucas a second chance? Write a short essay explaining your opinion. Use information from the text, as well as supplemental online or library research, if needed, to make your argument in support of the neighbor or the animal control officer.

4. **Text Type: Narrative.**

    How might *Bella's Story* be different if Lucas was the narrator? With canine character Bella as the narrator, we learn how Bella discovers that Lucas is the person she is meant to be with no matter what, and the struggles she goes through to be with him. How would *Bella's Story* look from Bella's *person's* point of view? In the character of Lucas, write a few paragraphs about a key event, or series of events, from

the story. (For example, bringing food and water to the stray animals in the crawl space; standing up to the demolition workers; meeting Bella; meeting Olivia and Audrey; bringing Bella home to Mom; convincing the animal control officer to let Bella stay; searching for Bella after she escapes from Aunt Loretta and Uncle José's yard; or reuniting with Bella.)

5. **Research & Present: Jobs in animal welfare.**
   The animal control officer in *Bella's Story* has to balance the needs and rights of people and animals. Special training is required to be an animal control or welfare officer. Invite students to do online or library research to learn more about this important job. (Hint: check out the National Animal Care and Control Association at www.nacanet.org.) Students might also want to research other jobs related to animal welfare, such as animal welfare veterinarian, animal cruelty investigator, animal shelter manager, pet adoption counselor, humane educator, or wildlife rehabilitator. Have students present their findings on a job (or jobs) related to animal welfare in a Power-Point or other multimedia presentation.

6. **Research & Present: Companion and service dogs for military veterans.**
   In *Bella's Story*, Bella ends up offering comfort and even inspiration to Lucas's mom, who is a wounded military veteran struggling to get back on track emotionally and physically after being injured on duty in Afghanistan. Although Lucas's mom and Bella come together by chance, there are organizations dedicated to training and pairing dogs (often from res-

cues or shelters) with veterans who can benefit from the support of a service or companion animal. Have students work in pairs or small groups to research an organization that pairs service or companion animals with military veterans. (Here are a few organizations students might check out: Pets For Vets at petsfor vets .com; K9s For Warriors at www.k9sforwarriors.org; and Patriot Paws Service Dogs at patriotpaws.org.) Ask students to present their findings in an oral presentation, supported by colorful visual and written aids.

Supports English Language Arts Common Core Writing Standards: W.3.1, 3.2, 3.3, 3.7; W.4.1, 4.2, 4.3, 4.7; W.5.1, 5.2, 5.3, 5.7; W.6.2, 6.3, 6.7; W.7.2, 7.3, 7.7

About the Author

Ute Ville

W. BRUCE CAMERON is the #1 *New York Times* best-selling author of *A Dog's Purpose, A Dog's Journey, A Dog's Way Home, A Dog's Promise,* the Puppy Tales books for young readers, and the Lily to the Rescue chapter books. He lives in California.

WBruceCameronKidsBooks.com